NO WINGS ON A COP

Cleve F. [illegible]ams

First Published 1953
Fiction House Press Edition July 2022

isbn 978-1-64720-621-5

Fiction House Press
www.FictionHousePress.com

CHAPTER ONE

THERE WAS A CORPSE on the table in the autopsy surgeons' room adjoining the morgue. The surgeon's deft fingers probed for the three slugs that had turned a captain of detectives into a corpse. Lieutenant John J. Shannon took a pull at a pocket flask to fortify his stomach. Outside, in the anteroom, reporters and cops buzzed like flies, but in here it was very quiet; only the faint metallic snick of the instruments as the surgeon laid them on the porcelain tray. Presently even that ceased and there was no sound at all.

The surgeon's face was tired, gray and disillusioned under the glare of the cone light. Shannon's was tired too, younger but just as bitterly cynical. He had a dark skin and very dark eyes and a big nose and a thick shock of pepper-and-salt hair that you somehow knew was peppered prematurely, not with age. A hard guy until you looked at his mouth. The mouth was a giveaway. It was as fine and sensitive as a woman's and it had to be deliberately twisted into either a snarl or a sneer to keep you from knowing how soft he was.

He watched the surgeon place the three slugs into a little envelope and lick the flap. It was like an official seal on a document of state. Shannon's eyes met the dead eyes of the man who had been his boss. Almost roughly he pulled the edge of the sheet higher. Then he and the surgeon went out into the bedlam of the anteroom.

Jack Runyon of the *Telegram* grabbed Shannon's arm "Tough on you, fella."

"Yes."

"But anyhow, at least it's something to know they got his killer."

"Yes."

"It *was* Duquesne, wasn't it?"

Shannon glanced briefly at the olive face of Acting-Chief George O'Meara. "O'Meara says so, doesn't he?"

O'Meara overheard him and gave him a dark smile. "Was that a crack, Shannon?"

"Maybe," Shannon said. He shook Runyon off, shouldered his way through the crush and went out the side door into the clammy, unclean coolness of the night.

Smog swirled, thick and acridly brown, around Civic Center, as if trying to stain and contaminate the pristine buildings. In the old days, before heavy industry had sprung up to pollute it with belching smokestacks, the fog would have been clean and odorless, bracing to breathe. Now it pressed down on you and choked you. It was a pervading corruption in your lungs, a stink in your nostrils. It brought tears to your smarting eyes, doubly obscuring your vision because of its irritant quality as well as its opaque heaviness that reduced visibility to less than a city block.

He scowled bleakly. "God damn it," he said in a bitter voice. Alone out here, he found that profanity brought little relief for the ache in his throat, the stuffiness in his chest. You couldn't dissipate the smog by cursing it, and besides, he knew that smog was not the cause of his tight throat and the leaden weight around his heart. "God damn it," he said again, angrily, letting slow rage rise up inside him like a cleansing fire. "What in the hell is the matter with me? Everybody has to die some time. Cops sooner than most."

He strode across the street to a bar and had two quick shots of rye. Two were all he usually needed to lift him out of his occasional moods of black Irish somberness, but tonight he had the feeling that two quarts wouldn't do it, let alone two drinks. The whiskey merely made him sullen.

Presently he left the bar, went over to the cab rank on the corner and rode down to his hotel. Upstairs, in his room, he lay on the bed, fully dressed, and stared at the ceiling. The skipper's dead face kept intruding and the dead eyes kept saying, "It was a frame, John J. They jobbed me."

"I know that," Shannon said, just as though Captain Grady were really there in the room with him. He didn't believe that the gambler Duquesne had shot the skipper; he didn't believe that Duquesne's five-grand check, found in the skipper's pocket, had come there with the skipper's knowledge. Nor with Duquesne's, for that matter.

After a while there was a knock on the door. "Come in," Shannon said. He didn't bother to get off the bed.

The door opened and Frances McGowan came in. Her eyes had an expression of distress, but in spite of this she was something to look at. You have looks and a shape or you don't get to model five hundred dollar gowns in the salons.

She moved gracefully across the room and sat down on the edge of the bed. "I just heard, Shan." Her voice was gentle.

He nodded.

"I knew how you'd be feeling," she said, and touched his hand. "I'm sorry."

"Thanks." He withdrew his hand from under hers.

She got up and walked over to the window. She had on a pair of silver foxes that would have set Shannon back a couple month's salary. "You don't want me here, Shan?"

"Sure. You smell nice." He saw her shoulders quiver ever so slightly at his intentionally barbed cynicism. "Don't mind me, hon. I'm a heel. Descended from a long line of heels." He eyed the smooth planes of her back, the neat curves. "Christ, I don't know what you see in me. I don't know why you bother."

She turned around and smiled at him. "Don't you?" Then she came back to the bed and pushed him a little with her palms. He rolled over, obediently, and buried his face in the pillows so that she could put her cool fingers on his neck, stroking, soothing, not saying anything.

Bye and bye he sat up. He felt relaxed, and his face was no longer cynical or sullen. "You'd better ring for a drink, kitten."

"All right."

While she was phoning, Shannon went into the bathroom and washed his face in cold water and combed his hair. When he came out he looked almost normal and the bellhop had come and gone. Fran was pouring the drinks, his straight, hers with ice and a little ginger ale. "What are you going to do, Shan?"

"I don't know yet." The straight rye tasted good to him, now. "I haven't had time to think." He held out his glass for a refill. "They're holding Duquesne for the kill."

"Yes, I know." She gave her attention to the job of pouring whiskey, not looking at Shannon. "Acting-Chief

O'Meara made an official statement to the papers and the networks." Her voice took on a flat, sing-song quality as though she were reading from an unseen press handout. "He hated to uncover what was bound to make a department scandal, but the check proved that Captain Grady had been extorting money from Duquesne, and that the murder resulted from this apparent shakedown. It is believed that Grady squeezed once too often and Duquesne got tired of it."

"It is believed," Shannon said, sourly mocking. "Sure. That's the way it was meant to look."

"But you don't buy it?"

"Grady never took a crooked dime in his life," Shannon answered harshly. "Not only that, but Duquesne is a square gambler; one of the squarest I've ever known. He didn't have to pay off because he's never had a squawk."

"Then what's behind it all, Shan?"

"Election's three days away," he said significantly. "I wish to hell Regan was in town."

"Where is he?"

Shannon's laugh was a short, mirthless sound. "At a police chief's convention up in San Francisco. A fine goddamned time to be horsing around like a Rotarian."

"Why don't you go to the mayor?"

"Maybe I will." He scowled darkly. "Trouble is, I haven't got a thing to go to anybody with. If those slugs they dug out of Grady check with Duquesne's gun, and I think they will, even if they have to fake it somehow, it's going to be his neck and nobody would believe him on a stack of Bibles."

Fran shook her head. "I don't get it."

"You and me, hon."

"But what does O'Meara stand to gain by all this?"

"That's something else that's over my head," Shannon said gloomily. He stood up and put on his hat. "I think I'll go down and have a talk with Duquesne."

"May I come too?"

He looked at her. "Don't be a fool, Fran. This is big stuff. The skippers dead and everybody in town knows what I thought of him. In my book he was God."

"Is that bad?"

"Now that he's dead, yes. Because the minute I start getting in anybody's hair I stand a good chance of being found dead too. I'm going to have to watch my step and I don't want to be worried about you."

She flared in sudden anger. "Well, isn't that fine! Isn't that just too, too dandy! *You* don't want to be worried about *me.* And just why do you suppose I came up here in the first place? Why do you think I'm always around under your feet? Because you're a second Einstein?"

"I wouldn't know." He shrugged. "All I know is I've got to handle this thing my way. For a while, at least. And my way is alone. If you feel like getting sore because I won't let you tag along, because I want to keep you out of the trouble I may be getting into, help yourself."

Her shoulders drooped. "All right. As long as you put it that way. As long as it's my safety you're thinking about. You liar," she added without rancor. At the door she turned, facing him and smiling. The smile was a little wry, a little tremulous at the corners of her lips. "You're so damned good to me I suppose I ought to get down on my knees and thank you."

"Cut it out hon."

The smile went away. "Would you mind kissing me just once Shan? You never have, you know."

"I never knew you wanted me to," he said. He bent and kissed her on the mouth. "Why didn't you tell me?"

"You're a fool, John J. Shannon."

He kissed her again, holding her tightly in his arms for a moment before letting her go. "Sure," he said easily. "All cops are fools. If they weren't they wouldn't be cops." Then they went downstairs and he put her in a cab.

It was eleven o'clock when he got back to Civic Center. The acrid smog was thicker and uglier than ever.

Floyd Duquesne was being held, temporarily, in one of the detention cells on the top floor of the Hall of Justice. Shannon rode up in the express elevator, went through the routine formalities at the jailer's desk, waited for the chrome-steel barred door to be opened for him, then strode along a white tiled corridor that was as clean and glistening as a hospital hallway. It even smelled antiseptic, like a hospital, although the odor of lysol vaguely reminded him of a cheap bawdy-house too.

Duquesne was a tall man, and very slender, and Shannon had never before seen him when he wasn't dressed in perfect taste: quietly unobtrusive but immaculate down to the minutest detail. Now, though, he was in shirt and pants, and there was sweat stains under his arms. He had been worked over, all right; you could see this, in spite of the fact that there wasn't a mark on his face. A session in the goldfish room doesn't necessarily leave bruises that show, which was something else Duquesne had learned the hard way. His gray eyes had the look of a caged eagle's, unwavering, bleak, watchful.

"Hello, Shannon."

"Hello," Shannon said. He watched the turnkey down at the far end of the corridor. "How are you? A rhetorical question," he added. "Requires no answer. I know how you are. Not so good."

"I'm getting by."

"It says here. They allow you to send for counsel yet?"

"O'Meara took a message," Duquesne lifted a shoulder. "Naturally I don't know whether he forwarded it."

"Who did you ask for?"

"Duffield."

"All right," Shannon said. "I'll see that you get him."

Duquesne's small mustache curved upward in a brief smile. "You will?"

"I said I would. I don't make empty promises. I'm not O'Meara."

"What's your angle, Shannon?"

"The skipper was a friend of mine. A damned good friend of mine. One of the best I ever had."

"And I'm supposed to have killed him," Duquesne said. "Or hadn't you heard?"

Shannon made rumbling sounds deep in his throat. "I could let them gas you."

"Or even help them a little, eh?"

"If I thought you'd done it I'd shoot you down right here and now," Shannon said. He would have, too. He waited until the stiffness went out of Duquesne's shoulders. "Where were you tonight?"

"Home. I told them that. I couldn't prove it, though."

"And was your gun home too?"

"It was and it still is as far as I know." Duquesne spread his fine, well-cared-for hands. "I'm not much of a gun-toter, Shannon. Never have been."

"I know that." Shannon curled strong fingers about the bright steel bars, leaned his face close, spoke a one-word question. "Lombardi?"

"What about Lombardi?"

"I asked you first. Don't fence with me."

"Then don't talk in riddles."

Shannon's eyes began to smoulder. "Christ!" he breathed. "Look, Floyd. You've been a thorn in the side of the gambling ring for a long time—"

"Have I? Why?"

"Because you wouldn't fall in line. Because, according to your lights, you played the game straight and gave the suckers an even break. It's Lombardi that's doing this to you, isn't it?"

"I wouldn't know, copper."

Shannon reflected angrily that he was up against the same old blank wall. These guys always figured they could take care of things themselves. As a rule they could, too, but there were exceptions. And this, he felt, was one.

"All right," he said with dogged patience, "we'll skip that a while. Let's talk about the check."

"Check?"

Shannon's neck reddened. "God damn it, stop parroting me like the straight man on a television comedy show. Was the check they found in the skipper's pocket on the level?"

"That I wouldn't know, copper."

"Was it yours?"

"They didn't let me see it, so how can I answer that? If you show it to me I might be able to tell you more about it. I'm not being evasive, Shannon. Just reasonable. Logical."

"Do you remember giving out a five grand check recently?"

"I cashed one at the bank about a week ago."

"How was it written?"

Duquesne made a thoughtful mouth. "I made it out to bearer because I expected to send somebody else after the money. Then I had to go downtown anyway, so I cashed it myself."

"Where do you bank?"

"The Third National."

There was a loud metallic clang down at the end of the tiled corridor, echoing along the distance like steely thunder in a tunnel. Shannon turned around, quickly. He saw O'Meara pounding hard heels toward him.

The acting-chief's darkly handsome olive face was flushed and his eyes were hard, antagonistic. "What the hell is the idea, Shannon?"

"I thought I'd work on the case a little. Mind?"

"What is there to work on?"

"Nothing, I guess," Shannon answered mildly. "I can see from the look on your face that the slugs checked with Duquesne's gun. You just got the ballistics report."

"You're God damned right. On both counts."

Shannon put his hands in his pants pockets so that O'Meara couldn't see how they were balled into tight, hard fists. He said, "Duquesne tells me he asked for Duffield as counsel. You send for him yet?"

O'Meara's eyes shifted. "I was just going to when I heard you were up here futzing around."

"Such language." Shannon clucked his tongue. "From an officer and a gentleman, too." He smiled with his mouth but not with his eyes.

"If that's another crack—"

"Perish the thought, pal. It was merely a figure of speech." Then, in a carefully casual voice, Shannon said, "Getting back to Duffield, I'll go with you while you send for him. That way I'll be sure of one thing at least."

"See here, Shannon, I don't like your tone!"

Shannon's smile became a leer. "Dear me, you mean I've offended you? And in front of your prisoner?" His black brows drew together. "Remind me to apologize."

O'Meara took a forward step, truculently. "Aren't you forgetting something, Shannon?"

"What? That you're acting-chief while Regan's away? No, I'm not forgetting it." Mockingly he saluted. "Lead on, Chief. I'm sure Duquesne isn't interested in our gay banter. Are you, Duquesne?"

The gambler had retired to the far side of his cell and was standing with his back toward them. He didn't answer.

O'Meara exhaled audibly. His nostrils flared a little and you noticed a rim of white around his tight mouth. Shannon decided that the guy was rummaging in his mind for the word "insubordination" but couldn't find it. He probably couldn't have pronounced it even if he had found it, Shannon thought. Or spelled it, either. A glint of feral amusement came into Shannon's veiled eyes as he and the acting-chief fell into step and went up the corridor together. Shannon did not bother to glance back at Floyd Duquesne in the detention cell.

At the desk, he let O'Meara check out for both of them. Going down in the elevator he could sense the acting-chief covertly watching him. Presently O'Meara spoke sotto voce, without moving his lips. "There's a captaincy open, Shannon."

"Yes, I know. Grady's berth until he vacated it tonight. Three bullets evicted him from it."

"He had that coming. He was overdue."

"You think so?"

"I know so. I know what the evidence shows. How would you like to be a captain Shannon?"

"I'd like it fine if it didn't make a heel out of me."

"Or maybe a corpse like Grady?"

They stepped out of the elevator. "Meaning exactly what?" Shannon said softly.

O'Meara let a sudden string of gutter oaths dribble from between his lips. "You shanty-Irish son of a bitch, how would you like to have me break you?"

"Well, it might prove something."

"Prove what, for instance?"

"It might prove that you're afraid of me. Are you?"

"Who, me?" O'Meara looked startled. "*Me* afraid of *you?* Hell, no!"

"That's nice," Shannon said. "Then I'll probably go right on being a cop for a while."

Shannon started to walk past the open door of the pressroom. Jack Runyon of the *Telegram* saw him and beckoned him with a limp copy of his paper, still damp from the presses. Shannon went in. A bunch of legmen from the other sheets were sitting around in a blue haze of cigarette smoke, theorizing as to what the murder would do to the administration. The consensus seemed to be that all hell was about to break loose. There was considerable speculation as to how many official heads would roll, on or before election day.

Runyon said, "Anything new, fella?"

"You tell me. You're the reporter."

"I get it. No comment, eh? Can I quote you on that?" Runyon shoved his copy of the *Telegram* at Shannon. "Oh, well, we've already got plenty of comments, for what they're worth. If they're worth anything." He waggled the paper.

"Stop clowning. I'm not in the mood." Shannon took the folded extra. A banner and a couple of sub-heads carried the main facts. The lead story was set three columns wide, in bold-face. There were the usual hastily engraved pictures. Below the fold, in a series of boxes, were statements by various officials.

Mayor Argyle: "I can't believe it."

District Attorney Jorgensen: "I have always found Captain Grady to be an efficient police officer. However, my office has been aware for some time that the metropolitan force has been honeycombed, if not by actual bribery, then by an amazing lack of cohesion bordering upon downright want of co-operation. Evidence furnished this office by the police department is frequently so incomplete that quite often successful prosecution is difficult, or, in some cases, impossible."

Acting-Chief O'Meara: "I could have followed the usual procedure and whitewashed a brother officer, but to me there is a higher duty. I shall probably be censured by certain men inside the department. Actually I believe my own life to be in danger for the stand I have taken, but regardless of personal jeopardy my oath of office demands a strict accounting to the public which pays my salary. I shall give it, let the axe fall where it may. It is most unfortunate for all concerned that Chief Ryan is not at his desk at this time."

•

A front page editorial pointedly commented on the fact that Captain Grady had been a close friend of the mayor and also of the absent chief of police. By innuendo you gathered that all three of them were tarred with the same stick and that it might not be entirely coincidence that Chief Regan was in San Francisco. The editorial writer had done a neat job of smearing, while avoiding any remarks that might be legally construed as libelous.

Shannon ripped the paper to shreds, threw them on the already littered floor. "You'd think the skipper was on trial instead of lying dead in the morgue! Christ!" He glared at the reporter, his eyes muddy. "What is this, anyway?"

"Election time," Jack Runyon said.

Shannon snorted in disgust, shouldered Runyon aside and went across the hall to the telegraph bureau. Here he sent a wire to Regan, up north:

"If you like being a police chief you had better get back here. John J. Shannon, detective-lieutenant." He then went over to City Hall, its white marble purity obscured by the pall of brown smog so that you could do little more than guess at the lights brightly gleaming from certain windows in an upper floor.

The spacious anteroom of the mayor's office, when he reached it, was as crowded as a department store bargain basement at nine in the morning. There were a dozen committeemen, a clucking little cluster of reformers, a bunch of lobbyists for the contractors, a couple of ministers and, over in one corner with a tight little clique of his own, Nick Lombardi. Shannon knew them all. A small silence fell as he walked in. He shoved through to one of the secretaries' desks and spoke to the tired-looking blonde behind it.

"Tell His Honor Lieutenant Shannon would like to see him." He didn't even try to lower his voice. The blonde looked scared for a minute, then as everybody started talking again she picked up a phone and said something into it. When she got her answer she said, "If you'll wait, Lieutenant?" Her voice sounded tired to match the weariness on her face.

Shannon nodded curt thanks, then smiled briefly at her to take the curse off his curtness. After all, he had no grudge against blondes. He had one against somebody else in the room, though. He went over and planted his feet in front of Big Nick Lombardi.

"My skipper never took that check."

"Ah, so?"

"Nor any other. And anybody says he did is a lying son of a bitch."

Lombardi looked at him, sleepy-eyed. He was fat-faced, slow moving, almost lethargic in his manner. It was rumored that he never got up before two in the afternoon and that he had to have somebody bathe him. He had shiny, crinkly black hair and eyes as soft and liquidly brown as a cow's. He smelled of lilac vegetal.

"No doubt you're right, Lieutenant." His voice was warm butter spread on velvet.

"You're goddamned right I'm right."

"Sure."

The two guys who acted as Lombardi's bodyguards deliberately turned their backs and faced the nearest window, pretending to be very interested in what was going on in the street ten stories below. If they saw what was going on in the street they had eyes equipped with radar to penetrate the smog. Shannon was not deceived. He knew they were watching him narrowly, using the window as a mirror.

The blonde secretary touched Shannon's arm, timidly. "The mayor will see you now, Lieutenant." He thanked her and went through the solid-paneled door.

Paul Shacklewood Argyle was not a large man, nor did he strike you as being a strong one. In private practice he had been an excellent attorney, not brilliant perhaps, but competent. His years in public office had done little to change this impression. The papers of the day quoted him occasionally on topics of the day, so that you knew there was a man named Paul Shacklewood Argyle in the mayor's office, but there had been no issues of vital importance to make him an outstanding figure. He had sandy hair and a short-clipped sandy mustache and he wore pince-nez. His desk was much too big, too ornate.

Shannon took off his hat, not out of respect but because it irked him. "What kind of a statement was that—you can't believe it?"

"It was a safe statement."

Shannon turned purple. "Safe! Christ, the guy was my friend, and your friend, and you sit there and talk about a safe statement! Who the hell cares?"

"You are talking to the mayor of this city," Argyle said.

"No kidding!"

Argyle's glasses glinted in the light and his rather fragile fingers played a little tattoo on the desk. "Just why did you come here, Lieutenant?"

Shannon took a deep breath and expelled it slowly, carefully, as though afraid that if he let it out all at once he would collapse like a punctured balloon. He went over to the window. "I seem to be bucking the whole town on this thing. Nobody gives a damn about a dead police captain, or how his reputation is slimed up with filth. All any of you can think about is how it's going to affect you."

"That's not quite fair."

Turning, Shannon put his two hands flat on the broad desk and said, "All right, even on that basis you can't afford to sit still and twiddle your thumbs. They'll pull you down, and they'll pull Chief Regan down with you. You think if they could frame that check on the skipper that they can't frame you? Already the papers are hinting a tieup, intimating that Regan is off the scene because he's afraid."

"What do you want, Shannon, a promotion?"

Shannon made an inelegant sound with his mouth. "The best you could do is make me a captain and I've already been offered that. I want the real killer of the Old Man and I'm going to tear this town apart to get him."

"You don't think Duquesne did it?"

"Do you?"

More drumming of fingers. "I don't know, Shannon. Honestly I don't." The brown eyes behind the pince-nez steadied on Shannon's face. "You see the spot I'm in about O'Meara, don't you?"

"Sure. You remove him as acting-chief and they'll say he was an honest cop trying to do his duty and you were afraid of what he'd uncover. Leave him in and he'll uncover something if he has to manufacture it first. Either way you're sunk. That's what this whole thing is about and it's the only reason I think you're an honest man. What do you owe Big Nick Lombardi?"

"Lombardi's votes put me in office."

"But you haven't panned out as good as he expected?"

"I don't know, Shannon. On the surface he's still friendly. It may be the opposition that is causing all this trouble. When someone wants to be mayor badly enough, or district attorney badly enough, almost anything is possible."

"The D.A. isn't worried."

"No Jorgensen isn't worried. He'll win, no matter what happens to me. In fact, he can use this police business to further his own ends. The city is all the opposition wants. They're not after the county."

Shannon nodded. "The big dough is in the city. Has Lombardi got anything on you?"

"No, I've done him what favors I could without its costing the taxpayers anything. Chief Regan has never had orders from me to lay off anything criminal."

"Lombardi ever ask you to?"

"He's asked me to speak to Regan a time or two. I told him Regan was handling the police department."

Shannon put on his hat. "Okay, I'll be seeing you."

"I hope so." Argyle let him get to the door before he added, "You sent a wire to Regan."

Shannon whirled. "Things certainly get around, don't they?"

"O'Meara didn't like it very well."

"So what did he suggest?"

"That you be suspended."

"Well, am I?"

"Not yet," Argyle said. "Just watch your step."

Shannon went out the side door, caught a down elevator and went over to the police garage and got into the car he always used. Nobody tried to stop him. At the far end, where the mechanics' benches were, a bunch of prowl cops were standing around a wrecked radio cruiser.

Shannon settled himself under his wheel, stepped on the starter and the whole world seemed to explode in his face.

CHAPTER TWO

THE WORLD BLEW UP with a bright orange-colored roar, sending Shannon hurtling headlong into a darkness that had no bottom. He became nothing in a void of nothingness. Then, a good deal later, the pain came.

His left arm hurt to beat hell. A sharp, stabbing ache coursed upward into his shoulder on little hot filaments, and there was a carbolic-acid smell in his nostrils. He opened his eyes to the white tile and porcelain brightness of an emergency operating room.

An interne was trying to pour something down his, Shannon's throat. "Drink it. It's good bonded whiskey. You're going to need it. You've got a broken left arm and we don't want you screaming like a banshee when we set it. Might drive away customers, you know."

"Great kidder," Shannon said. "I'll bet you get a hell of a kick out of funerals." He drank, grimaced. "Who called that rotgut bonded?" It had a bitterness that overrode the sourmash flavor, and he wished dismally that he could have had a pony of nice clean rye for a chaser, to take the astringent taste out of his mouth. It occurred to him that the interne had double crossed him, and that the bitter flavor was because the bourbon had been adulterated with a barbiturate to put him to sleep.

The interne held an X-ray negative to the light, studying it. The large rectangle of film was still wet. Shannon mumbled: "I hope they caught the natural expression of my clavicle when they made the snapshot." Then he closed his eyes, and the interne seized his left wrist and gave it a yank. Sweat popped out on Shannon's forehead as he felt the bone-ends grinding together. He was suddenly glad that the whisky had been dosed with pain-killer.

"You were pretty lucky, copper," the interne said.

Shannon said, "Yes," and went drifting down into bottomless darkness again.

Presently the darkness lightened to misty gray, so that he was aware that his arm had now been set and splinted. A male nurse was industriously mixing up a batch of what looked to be cement, for all the world like a plasterer's assistant, and handing it to the interne, who was the plasterer. The interne lifted Shannon and swung him around, letting him sit on the edge of the table with his legs dangling over the side.

"Hurt very much, copper?"

"Enough."

"Be finished in a minute now."

It seemed like a hell of a long minute. Sweat rolled down into Shannon's eyes, stinging them, while the interne completed his job on the arm and finally hung the arm in a sling deftly tied around Shannon's neck. Shannon never said a word.

Bye and bye the nurse brought another drink. "Doc's all done with you, Lieutenant. Here, have a little snort. You deserve it. You're quite a guy."

"The hell with it. The hell with you, too."

"It's straight stuff this time. See, I'll prove it." He drank it himself, then poured a replacement from a brown fifth. "Drink hearty."

Shannon sniffed and sipped suspiciously. There was no bitter taste, he found. He polished it off. "Much obliged. Is it all right for me to go now?"

"Better lie down and rest a while," the interne said. "There's a bed in the next room."

"No. Thanks just the same, but no," he answered firmly. "Just get me my coat and help me on with it. I've got people to see and things to do."

The nurse wagged his head. "What a man."

The street door opened and Captain O'Meara came running into the room with Jack Runyon and a couple of other reporters. "What happened, Shannon?"

"Somebody gave me a trick cigar," Shannon said. He slid off the edge of the white table, wobbled over to a mirror and looked at his face. There wasn't a mark on it. The eyebrows weren't even singed. "I thought explosions did things to you."

The interne said, "The steering wheel hit you in the heart. That's what knocked you out. You broke your arm falling out of the car afterward."

"Imagine that." He looked around the room. "I wish to Christ somebody would find me my coat so I can get out of here." He let his eyes rest on Captain O'Meara. "You publish the story in your own way, Chief. I don't know what happened. I just got in the car and stepped on the button and the thing went bang."

"That's all you can tell me?"

"Yes."

"Or could it be that you don't care to tell me any more?"

"It's all I know about it, except that it's a very funny joke on somebody."

"What do you mean by that?"

"I only busted an arm. I should have broken my neck." He turned to the male nurse. "How long have I been here?"

"About an hour all told. Right, Doc?"

"More like an hour and a half," the interne said.

Shannon said, "That's too long. My coat, please."

The interne frowned. "You're not being very smart, copper. I really think you ought to rest a while."

"Why? I'm not tired. I feel swell." Curiously enough, he did, too. His arm throbbed a little, like a toothache after the novocaine has been jabbed in, but aside from this he deemed himself in excellent shape, everything considered. He saw a closet door and opened it and found his coat and hat. The interne reluctantly helped him into the coat. Shannon, standing before the mirror, put on the hat himself, adjusting it to the precisely correct angle. He decided that he looked very jaunty indeed. "Well, I'll be seeing you guys. Thanks for everything." He walked out.

He went up to the mayor's office. The same gang was still in the anteroom, the same tired blonde was at the desk and the same little silence fell when he came in, only this time everybody looked at the bulk of his broken arm instead of his face. The blonde seemed upset by it. The reformers looked fascinated, the lobbyists speculative, the ministers appalled. The blonde appeared to be on the verge of asking him what had happened, then changed it to an uncertain, "The mayor is engaged just now, Lieutenant. I'm not sure he will be able to see you."

"That's all right," Shannon smiled at her. He then walked directly across the room until he stood in front of Nick Lombardi. Without saying anything he made a fist of his right hand and smashed Lombardi in the mouth.

One of the two bodyguards was very fast with his gun. He had it out and shoved in Shannon's belly almost before the sound of the blow had died away in the room's shocked silence. "You son of a bitch."

Lombardi touched an immaculate handkerchief to a drop of blood on his lips. "Never mind, Sticky."

Sticky put his gun away with an air of frustration. "Hell, Nick, it would be self-defense, wouldn't it?"

"Forget it?"

"There's a whole office full of witnesses that the bastard asked for it."

"I said to let it go, Sticky."

Shannon sneered at the bodyguard. "You heard what the man said. He said to let it go. When the man says something, do it. He's Big Nick Lombardi. He carries weight in this town."

"That he does. You're crowding your luck, copper."

"After what happened to me a couple of hours ago I don't have to crowd my luck. I bear a charmed life. Pull that gun on me again and I'll prove it to you. I'll take it away from you and shove it down your goddamned throat."

The guy did not pull his gun a second time. You knew he wanted to, but Lombardi's soft cow-like eyes warned him against it.

One of the ministers came over. "He who lives by the sword shall die by the sword."

"You hear that, Shannon?" Lombardi asked liquidly.

"I hear it," Shannon said. "But at least a sword is clean." He turned and strode past the blonde at the desk and went to the door of the mayor's office. He opened it without knocking and walked in. Paul Argyle was just hanging up a telephone. There was a man seated in the chair alongside Argyle's ornate desk, a large and florid man in impeccable tweeds.

This was Police Chief Regan.

Regan stood up and regarded Shannon with astonishment. "Good God, Lieutenant, why aren't you in the hospital?"

"Some of the newspapermen phoned me," Paul Shacklewood Argyle added quickly, by way of explaining how he and Regan had already known about Shannon's injury. "They called me up right after the thing happened. Or right after you were taken in for emergency surgery. I must say I'm surprised to see you up and around and looking so remarkably, er, undamaged except for the arm."

"I'll bet you're surprised." Shannon bared his teeth in what could have been a smile. "You and some other people. Including Nick Lombardi." Before the mayor could question him as to the meaning of this remark, Shannon turned to Regan. "Hello, Chief."

Vern Regan took Shannon's right hand and gripped it. "By God, I'm glad to see you, John J." He scowled. "I was worried. The way His Honor and I heard it, you were in bad shape." His sharp eyes, the color of clear blue lakes, inspected Shannon searchingly. "Are you sure you're all right? Are you sure you shouldn't be in bed taking it easy?"

"You wouldn't want that, would you, Chief?"

"Hell no, not if you're able to navigate. We can't afford to lose the services of a man like you. Not if it can be avoided. Especially at a time like this."

Shannon found a loose cigarette in his pocket, put it in his mouth and let Mayor Argyle light it for him. He dragged the smoke deep into his lungs, exhaled through his nostrils. "At a time like this you can't afford to lose the services of any decent police officer. But you lost Captain Grady."

"That's why I flew down from San Francisco as soon as I heard the news," Regan said soberly.

"You got my wire?"

"Wire? What wire? No."

Argyle said, "He wired you to hurry south if you wanted to keep on being chief of police," and smiled as if this were absurd. "He seemed to think there would be a shakeup."

"A shake-out," Shannon amended.

Regan rubbed a hand along his clean-shaven cheek. "I appreciate your loyalty to me, Lieutenant. I won't forget it."

"But my concern over your keeping your job was unnecessary, eh?"

The mayor answered that. "Entirely unnecssary, Shannon. I've no intention of relieving Chief Regan from his duties. As long as I remain in office, so does he."

"A three-day assurance," Shannon said. "Until election After that, what?"

"Let's cross our bridges as we come to them," Regan said. "As far as I'm concerned, Mr. Argyle will win in a landslide."

"In spite of a murder and an alleged bribery scandal stinking up his administration's police department?"

Argyle said smoothly, "That may be a blessing in disguise." A flush crept into his cheeks as Shannon glared at him. "I'm afraid I put that very badly. Nobody regrets Captain Grady's death more than I do. I regarded him as a close personal friend as well as an efficient law officer. But—"

"But it was a blessing when somebody pumped three bullets into him," Shannon's voice was not quite a snarl.

"You misunderstand," Argyle fluttered his hands on the desk. "I merely meant that if there's corruption in the department this brings it out into the open where we can do whatever must be done to correct the condition."

Vern Regan nodded. "I've already ordered a thorough investigation of departmental personnel, John J. If we find crookedness it will be punished. The top brass has nothing to hide. I've said so to the newspapers."

"Well, that makes capital of Grady's murder," Shannon rasped. "It turns his corpse from a political liability to an asset even though it smears his reputation all to hell. Who cares about a dead man's good name?" He grinned. "I'll bet you didn't think up that particular piece of weasling, Chief. It sounds more like His Honor, here."

The red in Argyle's face deepened. "Now, now, Lieutenant, I must again remind you—"

"That you're the mayor of this fair city. Yes. And you're determined to stay mayor when the votes are in and counted."

Very Regan cleared his throat. "He's done a good job in his first term, John J. Why shouldn't he want to be re-elected? Hell, Grady's death won't cost the Argyle administration any votes. In fact, he can point to the inherent honesty of the police force—its efficiency, too. After all, Grady's murderer was captured inside a couple of hours."

"You mean Floyd Duquesne was captured inside a couple hours."

"Isn't that saying the same thing?"

"What do you think?"

Regan lifted an eyebrow. "I wasn't in town when it happened. I'm in no position to form opinions. All I can do is accept the facts as presented."

"As presented by O'Meara, eh?"

"Well, he's in charge of the case." Regan looked a little uncomfortable. He cast a glance at the mayor, who avoided his eye. "He's running the department during my absence."

"He *was* running it during your absence. You're not absent now. You're present."

"Only temporarily."

Argyle murmured, "Chief Regan is flying back north to his convention as soon as he can clear a plane reservation."

"What?" Anger flared up in Shannon. "God damn it, Chief, you can't do that!"

"Why not? What's wrong with it? I hurried home when this thing broke, didn't I? I scotched the talk that I was afraid to show myself. I've issued statements to the reporters, I've ordered a full investigation of the department, I've done everything a man in my position ought to do."

Shannon's jaw took on a stubborn set. "Except take personal charge. A captain of detectives was killed. And an attempt was made to kill a detective lieutenant. Me. I'm not complaining about that part. But Grady's murder—"

"Is in competent hands," Argyle smoothly fielded the sentence.

"Meaning O'Meara's?"

"Yes."

Shannon looked at Regan. "You call O'Meara competent?"

"Let's not indulge in personalities," the chief said. "You've had your petty differences with Captain O'Meara, but after all he *is* acting-chief when I'm away. Try to get along with him, Shannon. For the good of the force."

"And for your own good as well," Argyle said.

"Would that be a threat, Your Honor?"

The mayor's glasses glinted. "I told you before that O'Meara suggested you be suspended from duty. I persuaded him that it was in the best interests of all concerned to let you stay on your job. When he thought it over he agreed that I was right. Chief Regan concurs in this opinion. He merely asks that you try to get along with O'Meara. I deem it sound advice."

"The trouble with you, Shannon, is you're upset," Regan said soothingly. "A friend of yours was murdered and you were bombed, all in one night. Right now your judgment may be a little warped. Go home and sleep on it, get some rest. You'll see things a lot differently in the morning. And if anything really important comes up you can always phone me long distance in San Francisco."

"So you really intend to duck out."

Regan seemed uncomfortable. Again his glance flicked toward Argyle and back again before he answered. You got the impression that he was talking and acting under hidden pressure, perhaps being obedient to orders he didn't quite approve of. It was a fleeting impression, though, and it was not reflected by his tranquil voice. "I'd stick around if I thought I could help, believe me I would. You know how I felt about Grady. But there's nothing I can do that you boys can't, and I'm scheduled to make a speech at the convention that would be awkward to get out of. Besides, I'll be in constant touch with City Hall here, and if I'm needed I can always fly back down in a couple of hours."

"In case of emergency," Argyle said in a tone that indicated he did not anticipate any such need. He stood up. "And now, Lieutenant, if you'll excuse me, I have a great deal to do. There are people who've been waiting to see me for hours, out there in the other room."

"Including Nick Lombardi," Shannon said. "Or has he already been in, given orders, gone out and come back again?"

Regan said, "Shannon!" rather sharply. Then he, too, stood up. "Well, I'll be running along, Paul. I guess we've discussed everything there is to talk about."

"Yes, I think so," the mayor said. He shook hands with the police chief. "I hope you make good connections to San Francisco." He merely nodded to Shannon. "Better get a little rest, Lieutenant. You've had a difficult time."

Shannon and Regan went out the side door. In the deserted corridor, Regan said, "Could I drop you anywhere?"

"Thanks just the same," Shannon refused.

The chief smiled crookedly. "I wish you'd quit thinking of me as a louse. I've always considered you a friend of mine."

"So was Captain Grady a friend of yours. Mine too."

"I'm not forgetting it."

"Neither am I," Shannon said coldly.

"While you're remembering, remember something else," Regan's eyes were steady. "I like my job, I want to keep it."

"So you're blowing town on Argyle's orders, because he wants to keep his, too. And he's Nick Lombardi's man."

"You could be wrong about that. The Lombardi part, I mean."

"Ah. Then Argyle did tell you to go back north."

Regan rubbed his cheek. "I won't discuss it with you, Shannon. What I will discuss is this. You've been damned loyal to me and I appreciate it."

"So you said."

"You think I've gone soft, don't you?"

"I used to think you had a hard core inside, like iron. If I had ever heard anybody call it a yellow streak I'd have hit him. I ouldn't now."

"Maybe I can convince you the iron core is still there; that it hasn't rusted or turned yellow. O'Meara wants to be chief of police. He might even be throwing in with the opposition. He has used the Grady kill to jockey Argyle into a corner, and my hands are tied for a little while. Do you know why I tried to warn you not to get too impertinent to His Honor a moment ago, not to push him too far?"

"You tell me."

"It goes back to what I just mentioned. Your loyalty to me."

Shannon looked at him.

"Suspended from duty, you could do me no good," Regan explained. "If you stay on the job, though, I know I've got somebody to look after my interests while I'm away. Someone I can depend upon. All right, to stay on the job you've got to stop needling Argyle. And you've got to get along with O'Meara, or at least pretend to. Is that plain enough?"

"Yes, with one proviso. I want it understood that I'm going to find out who killed Captain Grady and to hell with all this political stuff."

"You're convinced Duquesne isn't the man?"

Shannon nodded. "He's no more guilty than I am, evidence and ballistics and O'Meara be damned. And Grady was no grafter. He's dead and he's being smeared. Duquesne is alive and being railroaded. I'm going to dig until I learn the real truth."

"That's what I want you to do. Only you can do it better from inside than outside, so stay on your good behavior with O'Meara and with Argyle. Is that understood?" He offered his hand.

Shannon shook it. "You've got a one-armed detective lieutenant working for you, Chief. For you—and for Captain Grady."

Lieutenant Gus Vogel was a round-bellied little man with a fat, pinkly cherubic face, pale blue eyes as naive and trusting as a child's, and a Cupid's-bow mouth that always seemed to droop a little at the corners, as though in perpetual apology for secret and purely imaginary naughtiness. He dressed shabbily, in keeping with his salary, and he owned the only derby hat in the department. This was a trifle small for him.

Currently he was masticating a wad of gum with bovine placidity and watching Shannon search Captain Grady's desk. "Well, now look, John J.," he remarked after a while. "There ain't no sense in you being dead too."

Shannon absently cursed him without looking up from what he was doing. He didn't know what he was looking for. It wasn't very likely that the skipper had known in advance that he was going to be killed and made provision for the apprehension and conviction of his murderer, but sometimes you find a lead where you least expect it. Although Shannon hadn't much hope of this, it was worth trying on routine principles.

"It seems to me like you're playing with dynamite, John J.," Vogel said.

"I've already played with it." Shannon finished the desk without finding a thing. He indicated his broken arm. "Remember?" The arm bothered him. It wasn't only the toothache pain of it now that the sedative and the whiskey had worn off, but the awkwardness of its bulk hung across his middle. Every time he moved he bumped it into something; and his nerves, already frayed, were jumpy. The vertical lines at the corners of his mouth had deepened in the past few hours and his eyes had a half-dazed look in them. They were circled, dark.

Vogel coughed apologetically. "I'm a funny guy, John J. Maybe you think I'm kinda dumb, only you're forgetting something. You're forgetting that I worked for the skipper as long as you."

"So what?"

Vogel's moon face turned beet red, like that of a sad infant getting ready to cry. "So I'm trying to tell you, John J., that if you need any help all you've got to do is say so and I'm with you. All the way."

Shannon stood up and made a fist of his good hand and lightly hit Vogel on the arm. It was as close as he had ever come to showing affection for the man. "I'm a heel, Gus."

"You ain't no such thing," Vogel said indignantly.

"Lots of times I've been a heel to you. I'm sorry."

"Sure, John J."

Neither man said anything more for a while. Shannon presently picked up a phone and called the municipal International Airport. The guy at the airport information desk told him the field was locked in because of fog and all planes were being re-routed to Glendale-Burbank. Shannon called there and asked about the next flight due in from San Francisco. It was scheduled to land in forty minutes but was running a little late and would arrive about an hour from now. Duffield, Floyd Duquesne's attorney, would be on that.

Vogel said, "Why do you want to see Duffield?"

"Because he's got one of the best minds in the country. I need that kind of a mind."

"He'll have to be a wizard if he springs Duquesne."

"The hell with Duquesne," Shannon said. "You and I could spring him in a minute if we wanted to. At least we could fix it so that any two-for-a-nickel shyster could spring him."

"How?"

"Maybe I'll show you after a while. Right now Duquesne is doing all right where he is."

Vogel blinked his mild eyes. "Seems to me a man in jail on a murder charge ain't doing all right any way you look at it. I know I wouldn't think I was doing very good if I was in his spot."

"Use your brains. Once on the streets again, Duquesne would be playing right into the hands of the guys who framed him in the first place."

Vogel's forehead wrinkled. "I don't see that. I don't see how you figure."

"Say he was turned loose; say he disappeared after that—for good. Would there be any doubt then that he was guilty? Not much there wouldn't? I'm a little surprised our friends haven't thought of it."

"O'Meara?"

There was a knock on the door and Shannon put a cautioning finger to his lips before he went over and unlocked it. Frances McGowan stood there looking at him.

"Well, aren't you going to invite me in?"

"I thought I told you to stay away from me."

She glanced at his broken arm. "You also told me you were going to handle this in your own way. I think it's a pretty poor way, if you ask me."

"I didn't ask you."

Sparks danced in her fine eyes, and there were tears, too. You knew she was hotly angry at Shannon and miserably worried about him. She tried to pass it off with a gay gesture. "Flattery will get you nowhere, Mister Shannon. Besides, I'll bet you're this churlish with all the girls." The gaiety was a thin veneer. It cracked, melted away. "Oh, Shan, what have they done to you?"

"Nothing compared to what I'll do to them." A couple of dicks going past in the hall looked at Fran curiously. "You'd better come in, hon," Shannon said. He closed and locked the door after her. "I wish to hell you hadn't come, though."

"When I heard about the bomb I couldn't stay away. I've been looking all over for you." She touched the plaster cast in its sling. "Is it bad, Shan? Does it hurt?"

"I broke it falling out of the car. It hurts a little but it'll heal."

"Shan, what can I do? May I take you home and put you to bed, or—or—"

Gus Vogel, hearing this, blushed like a schoolboy. You knew from his expression that the idea of an unmarried and beautiful girl taking an unmarried man to her home and putting him to bed was profoundly disconcerting. Vogel was obviously embarrassed for Fran. It was equally obvious that he was casting about in his mind for a means of changing the subject before Shannon could take her up on her offer. Apparently Gus thought that a broken arm would be a very trivial obstacle to a guy like Shannon if he decided to go on the make.

Vogel stood up quickly on his short, thick legs and put his derby on so that he could make the polite gesture of taking it off again. "How do you do, Miss McGowan?"

"Hello, Gus."

He said, "Now look, Miss McGowan, about this place of yours you work at. What I want to know is—"

Shannon yelled at him. "For Christ's sake what is this, a coffee klatch?"

"I think he was trying to protect my honor," Fran said. "Weren't you, Gus?"

"Well, now," Vogel said uncomfortably.

"You've got an idea that Shannon is a roue. You want to know something? The psychologists claim that when one man suspects another of something like that, it's because of his own inhibited libido." Fran was using Vogel for a foil, teasing him to relieve her own tensions. "Which means," she added, "that at heart you're nothing but a lecher, yourself."

Vogel looked shocked. "I am not!"

"For God's sake!" Shannon said. He pushed Frances down into a chair. "When are you going to get it through your head that I meant what I told you? I'm poison. I'm a walking target any time I show myself from now on. You've simply got to stay away from me, kitten. Far away."

She studied him curiously. "I can't make up my mind about you, Shan. You're either being very smart, or crazier than usual. Either way you're worrying me sick. First somebody planted a pineapple in your car. Then they tell me you punched Big Nick Lombardi on the mouth in front of a dozen witnesses."

"One cancels the other," he said, scowling.

"I see. A cut lip for a broken arm." Her legs were sleek and tapered and very attractive in sheer gray nylon as she stretched them out in front of her. "It looks to me as though you got cheated. What makes you think Lombardi tinkered with your car?"

"I don't think he did. Not personally, anyway."

"Then why did you hit him?"

Shannon had been pacing up and down the room. Now he stopped. "Look, hon. Lombardi has more or less run this town for years. Guys like Floyd Duquesne and Chief Regan have been making it tough for him here lately, and Mayor Argyle hasn't turned out as well as he expected. With election less than three days away Lombardi has two choices. He can use this mess to break Argyle and put the opposition man in office, or he can use it to make Argyle listen to reason."

"Which alternative do you think he's taking?"

"I don't know. I'm almost inclined to suspect he's putting the screws on Argyle. There's no proof, but little things point that way. Things like Regan being away, and coming back for a couple of hours and then flying north again to that god-damned convention. I don't think Regan really wanted to go; he acted as though he had been given orders. Argyle is the only one who could manage that, I feel certain. And yet I may be talking through my hat. There's one thing I *am* sure of. O'Meara wants to be chief."

Fran's gray eyes were thoughtful. "So you punched Lombardi and that fixed the whole complex mess."

"That was insurance. If anything else happens to me, people will remember that I pasted Big Nick in the mouth and they'll wonder if maybe he didn't do something about it. He may do something anyway, but he'll have to be pretty damned careful."

She looked at him. "That was smart, Shan."

"Sure it was smart. See me preening myself? But what good will my smartness do me if you keep tagging me around? If they find out how much I—if they think I know you they'll cop you off and use you for leverage to stop me."

She stood up. Her eyes were shining and there was a tiny wistful smile on her lips. "That's the closest you ever came to telling me anything worth while, Shan. Be careful, will you?"

"Take her home, Gus," Shannon said.

"Well now, look," Vogel demurred. "First I've got to know where you're going to be." He rolled his eyes at Frances. "He is a very trying guy, Miss McGowan."

"Very trying indeed," she agreed. She touched Shannon's good arm. "Did you find out anything about that business down in the garage?"

"No."

"Have you tried to?"

"Of course. There are around four thousand men in the department who have access to that garage. Any one of them could have done it."

"Then what are you going to do?"

"I'm going to work on Floyd Duquesne's five-grand check, the one they found in the Old Man's pocket."

"Have you anything to go on?"

"A start. Duquesne cashed that check himself. Somehow it got out of the bank without being stamped."

"Her eyebrows lifted. "That sounds incredible. Not to say impossible."

"Nothing is impossible. I've got a fairly good idea how it was worked."

"Well?"

"Nick Lombardi is on the Third National board of directors."

CHAPTER THREE

THERE WAS NO GROUND FOG out in the Valley. The low clouds over Metropolitan Airport obscured the tops of the surrounding hills and gave a feeling of dampness to Glendale and Burbank, but it was a clean dampness, not tinctured by the stink of downtown smog. Shannon paced the concrete promenade between the administration building and the fabricated steel fence which enclosed the landing field, glancing up occasionally at the thick shroud of gray cotton batting that rode the breezeless night sky.

The airport was pretty much deserted. After three in the morning the sighseers are usually in bed and it was a safe bet that those who were left had business here. Shannon was startled to see Sticky, the fast gun who belonged to Big Nick Lombardi, come out onto the ramp from the lobby waiting room.

Sticky didn't see Shannon at first. He was a tall, lanky guy with a thin, down-curving mouth, very natty in a double-breasted Chesterfield. He sought the shadows beside one of the closed novelty shops and just stood there quietly.

Shannon strolled over to him, just as quietly. He said, "Hello, pal."

"Hello, there," Sticky said. He didn't seem a bit put out y Shannon's presence. "Not much doing tonight, is here?"

"I hadn't noticed. I've been pretty busy, myself."

Sticky looked at the empty left sleeve of Shannon's overcoat. "How's the arm?"

"Fine." They were just two casual acquaintances passing the time of day. You would never know that a little more than an hour ago one had been ready to shoot the other for punching his boss in the mouth. Shannon glanced aloft as he heard the drone of a plane. He couldn't see the ship, but its sound was intensifying as it came down through the overcast. Presently its wing lights would break through. "Meeting somebody?"

"Unh-unh. I just like to watch them come in."

"At this hour of the morning?"

"Any time. They sort of fascinate me. I'm going to jockey one of those things around some day myself."

"If you really want to do that," Shannon said, "you hadn't better pull a rod on me again."

Sticky yawned. "Next time I pull one it'll probably go off. I hope you're not in front of it." He flicked a pocket lighter aflame and touched it to his dead cigar. His mouth was faintly smiling but his eyes were cold. "Well, nice seeing you again." He turned his back and moved along the fence.

Presently Flight Eleven, a shiny four-engine job, came gliding down out of the clouds with its landing lights brooming the field. It touched earth, rolled a little way, swept around in a graceful curve and squatted on the tarmac, its idling props making circular glints of silver and then dying to stillness.

Sticky moved forward into the light, watching the pilot and co-pilot get out, and then one of the stewardesses, and finally four or five passengers. Ward Duffield limped down the steps and came through the gate, carrying a brief-case.

Shannon stepped forward. "Duffield."

The lawyer paused. He had a club foot and he favored this a little as he walked. It was his only distinguishing feature. The rest of him was inconspicuous, a sort of monochrome of gray. Even his face seemed without color. His voice was resonant, pleasant, not at all the flamboyant actorish voice you might expect of a noted criminal pleader. "Yes?"

"I'm Shannon, Headquarters."

"How do you do." It was polite, impersonal. It was four words to say while waiting for the opening move in a chess gambit. You got no more from the inflection than from the phrase itself.

Shannon said, "I'd like to ride in with you."

"All right." They went into the rotunda and got the attorney's suitcase. Shannon, carrying this, led the way to the exit, looked around and flagged a cab. The guy Sticky, he noticed, had disappeared. Shannon motioned his companion into the taxi first, then followed. As the cab got under way he could feel Duffield's eyes on him. Bye and bye Duffield said, "Official escort?"

"Not exactly," Shannon answered. He couldn't tell whether or not he was going to like this guy. He had seen him in court, knew him for a legal magician, but of the man himself he knew nothing. He got out a pack of cigarettes, offered it.

Duffield accepted one without comment. Shannon flared a kitchen match on the thumbnail of his good hand, tried not to indicate how pleased he was with the feat, lit the lawyer's cigarette and one for himself and flipped the match out the window just before it scorched his fingers. The two men smoked in silence for a couple of minutes. Then Shannon moved his shoulders irritably. "You a friend of Duquesne's?"

Duffield gravely considered this. "Why?"

"Hell's fire, don't you ever talk out of court? What kind of a guy are you, anyway?"

"I'm Floyd Duquesne's counsel."

"I didn't mean that."

"Duquesne is supposed to have shot a policeman. You are a policeman. It's rather obvious, isn't it?"

Shannon said a four-letter word. "Look, mister, I'm the guy that helped get Duquesne's hurry call through to you."

"Why?"

"I know Duquesne didn't kill Captain Grady and I want the guy that did kill him. Is that plain enough?"

Duffield studied him out of the corners of his eyes. "You have proof?"

"Nothing concrete." Shannon told him of the things that had happened.

"None of that is proof, my young friend."

"All right. I said there was nothing concrete," Shannon grated. "All I've got is absolute faith in my skipper's honesty. If that check they allegedly found in his pocket was sour then it's dollars to doughnuts that the rest of the setup is sour, too. Will you do something for me?"

"That depends on what it is you want?"

"Will you leave Floyd Duquesne in the can?"

"I probably couldn't do anything about it either way," Duffield said slowly. "I've been in touch with a source or two down here and I understand that Duquesne's gun matches up on a ballistics comparison with the slugs they took out of the body. Granting this to be true, you ought to know that you don't spring a man in the face of that kind of evidence."

"Play ball with me, counsellor, and I'll prove the evidence was phony."

"You think you can?"

"Yes."

"Then why don't you do it now?"

"Because I don't want Floyd Duquesne on the streets, God damn it. If he turned up missing, all the evidence I could collect or frame wouldn't mean a thing. He'd be guilty, period."

"Perhaps you're right." Duffield threw out his cigarette and turned to face Shannon. "You have a personal motive in this, over and above your natural feeling about Grady's death?"

Shannon tapped his plaster cast. "Very personal I've got a broken arm that could just as well have been my neck, and I'm a vindictive son of a bitch when it comes to people trying to kill me."

"Very well," Duffield said, "I'll play with you for a day or two. We won't even make an attempt to spring Duquesne."

"Thanks. That's a favor to me, and it's a bigger favor to Duquesne. When you talk to him I hope you can make him realize it. Make him see he's a hell of a lot safer where he is than he'd be on the outside."

Duffield nodded. "I don't suppose you'd care to tell me the name of the person you really suspect of murdering Grady?"

"I haven't got that far—yet. When I do, you'll know it. Until then, don't ask me to name names. I'd a hell of a lot sooner listen while you tell me what you think."

Duffield smiled. "I'm like you, Shannon. I don't know—yet. You'd scarcely expect me to have formed an opinion on so little tangible information."

"All right, skip it. Just so we know where we stand." The cab drew up before the Hall of Justice and Shannon got out, waited while the lawyer paid the fare. There was quite a crowd on the steps and inside the entrance lobby of the building. Shannon and the lame man went in.

Sighting Duffield, a dozen reporters swarmed down upon him. A sort of expectant hush fell as their spokesman said, "Looks as if you won't be needed after all, Counsellor."

"Meaning what?"

"Haven't you heard? Your client just escaped."

Shannon, hearing of Duquesne's escape, felt as if an unseen sledgehammer had hit him on the chest. The thing was impossible. Nobody could crash out of the detention cells up on the tenth floor. It simply couldn't be done, he told himself. Not without collusion on the part of someone on the inside. When he thought of this, a cold rage grew within him so that it hurt him even to breathe.

All Duffield said was, "Indeed?" as the reporters mobbed him to amplify the news. Then he looked silently at Shannon.

Shannon was immediately surrounded by guys demanding comment for the late morning editions. He had no comment to give them. Finally, when he couldn't stand the jabbering and chattering of the newspapermen any longer, he elbowed past them and climbed the steps and went up to Acting-Chief O'Meara's office.

Up here there was a crowd, too. O'Meara was at his desk, very commanding, very businesslike, very busy with three or four telephones. Over on the side of the room a turnkey was slumped in a chair and a couple of dicks were giving him rough and ready first aid. The turnkey had a lump on his forehead the size and color of a walnut, and there was a deep gash in the top of his bald head. He was sobbing hysterically, each sob ending in a hiccup. He looked as if he might be suffering quite a bit of pain.

Shannon walked grimly past the guy and approached O'Meara's desk with demanding questions boiling to his lips. O'Meara beat him to the punch by hanging up two of the phones and snarling in a loud voice, "Did you have anything to do with this?"

Shannon's jaw dropped. "Me?"

"You, by God. I asked you a question. Answer it."

By an effort so great that it drained all the blood from his face, Shannon swallowed the hot retort that swelled in his throat. He stared at O'Meara, then looked about the office. Everyone seemed to be studying him with a mixture of awe and disgust. Jack Runyon of the *Telegram* deliberately turned his back.

Color came back to Shannon's cheeks in a crimson flood. "The question doesn't deserve an answer, O'Meara."

O'Meara violently banged the desk with his clenched fist. "No more of your lip! You've been bucking me all the way on this thing, Shannon. You sent a wire to Chief Regan. You went over my head to Mayor Argyle. You intimated that we arrested the wrong man, then you went up and got chummy with the man himself. Now the man is gone and I'm asking you pointblank what you had to do with his escape."

"I had nothing to do with it."

"Where have you been this last hour and a half?"

"I've been out to the airport!" Shannon yelled.

"Why? What for?"

"I was meeting Duffield if you've got to know."

A little smile flicked over O'Meara's lips. His eyes were triumphant as he looked around the room. "You see? You hear that?" he said to nobody in particular but everyone in general. "Here is a man who professes great friendship for a dead superior and great sorrow over the superior's murder, yet he flagrantly and openly consorts with the murderer and with the murderer's attorney." His eyes bored into Shannon's, and Shannon saw the cruelty, the savagery, in them. He had seen the same expression in the eyes of a victorious prize fighter about to deliver a knockout to a beaten and helpless opponent. "I'm trying to be very fair, Lieutenant," O'Meara said.

Shannon's voice sounded thick, even in his own ears. "So I've noticed." He looked at the battered turnkey. "What happened, Pop?"

The guy tried to talk but coudn't.

O'Meara said wearily, "Never mind. If you had seen who conked you, all this wouldn't be necessary." He glanced obliquely at Shannon. "Still trying to be fair, Lieutenant, I'll repeat what happened. We had Duquesne down for questioning again and he was left in one of the detention rooms for a minute with only the turnkey for a guard. Somebody sneaked up behind the turnkey and knocked him out and Duquesne just vanished." He sneered. "I hope you can prove you were at the airport. Which airport?"

Duffield came in, his club foot making little clumping sounds on the bare floor. "Glendale-Burbank," he said. "And he can prove it." He looked around. "I hope I am sufficiently well known to all you gentlemen so that my word will be enough?"

"Of course, Counsellor," O'Meara said. He was making no direct accusation of complicity against Duffield. Shannon had a flash of insight which told him that O'Meara was actually afraid of the gray-clad, gray-haired, gray-faced attorney. O'Meara said: "I suppose you'll be going back north in the morning?"

"No," Duffield said, and this seemed to shake O'Meara a little. "No, I shall stay down here for a day or two."

"But what for? You don't expect your client to walk back into custody now that he's gone, do you?"

Shannon grabbed at that. "Seems like a damned funny attitude for you to take, O'Meara. Where's your confidence in the department? Surely you've got a dragnet out for Duquesne. But you sound as if you felt pretty certain in your own mind that the guy will never be picked up —alive. What makes you so cock-sure his disappearance is permanent?"

"Why, I—I'm not sure at all," O'Meara's neck got very red. "I mean how the hell do I know whether we'll nab him again?"

Duffield said, "In case Duquesne *is* picked up I should appreciate hearing from you. I'll be at the Corinthian." He turned and clumped out without looking at Shannon.

There was a brief silence. O'Meara broke it. "I didn't like that remark you made, Lieutenant. Were you implying that I've got secret knowledge of what's going to happen to Floyd Duquesne now that he's out?"

"I didn't imply anything. I can't help what you inferred."

"I see." Heavy lids lowered to veil the acting chief's smoky eyes. "Maybe I misinterpreted your meaning." He paused. "Well, is there anything else on your mind?"

"None you could answer without putting your heinie in a sling," Shannon said deliberately.

You could hear a chorus of indrawn breaths around the office. O'Meara stood up. "I think I'll have to ask you for your badge, Shannon."

"I was going to turn it in anyway," Shannon said. "I'm not very proud of being a cop any more." He fumbled the little leather case out of his pocket and placed it on the desk. "Goodnight, gentlemen—and Captain O'Meara." He pivoted and walked from the room.

He kept walking, down the stairs and through the lobby and onto the quiet street. The smog had lifted, as if with the lifting of Shannon's detective-lieutenant's shield, and he found that he could breathe the air with no discomfort. He went slowly around the block, thinking. Then, presently, he retraced his steps and headed for the police laboratory.

This was a series of cluttered-looking rooms on the top floor of the Hall of Justice. At four-thirty in the morning almost everyone had gone home and Shannon was hoping that the two technicians who were left had not yet heard about his dismissal. You can't get much cooperation from a police lab unless you're entitled to it. He pushed through the swing gate in the long counter and dropped into a chair, watching Ziggy Ziegler, the little ballistics wizard, play with his microscopes.

Ziegler looked up. "Hello, Lieutenant." He had a face only a mother could love, or even tolerate. At one time he had been a bantamweight fighter, not a very successful one, and each one of his features was a record of his various failures to duck when the other guy swung on him. "How's tricks?"

"Tricks," Shannon said, "are just swell." He made a great business of lighting a cigarette one-handed. He was getting pretty good at this. Ziegler didn't offer to help him. To Ziegler a trivial thing like a broken arm was not even a minor injury.

Shannon said, carefully casual, "Who turned the bullets out of Grady over to you, Ziggy?"

"O'Meara. Why?"

"I just wondered. I saw them taken out." Shannon took a deep drag on his cigarette before he added, "They were still in a sealed envelope, of course?"

Ziegler bridled. "What the hell is this? You think I don't know my own business? Certainly they were in a sealed envelope!" He spat on the floor. "Three slugs, and so what?"

"All right. Am I arguing?" Shannon got up and wandered around the room. The other technician put on his hat and went out, announcing that he was going for a cup of coffee. Shannon looked at Ziegler. "As I remember, it seems to me it was Captain Grady who gave you your first real chance in the department."

"Well?"

"You ought to feel almost as bad about him as I do."

"Maybe." They stared at each other for a while. Finally Ziegler said, "What's your angle, Shannon?"

Shannon adjusted his arm in its sling. "The envelope could have been switched. I didn't see the autopsy surgeon put any identifying marks on it."

"O'Meara put them on."

"He could have put them on another envelope, couldn't he?"

Ziegler fiddled nervously with things on his table. "Shannon, you're playing with dynamite."

Shannon tapped his broken arm and nodded.

"What's more, you're asking me to play with it," Ziegler said. He shrugged irritably. "They bring me a gun and three bloodstained slugs. I match them. They compare. That gun fired those slugs. My responsibility ends right there."

"Does it?" Shannon said gently.

Ziegler wiped sudden beads of sweat off his forehead. "Damn it, Shannon , what do you want?"

Shannon dropped his cigarette to the floor and put a heel on it. "I have the feeling that the skipper wasn't killed just to frame Duquesne. The frame was an afterthought. I believe Captain Grady had something and was murdered on account of it."

"But the slugs and the gun checked, I tell you!"

"Sure they did. But the slugs you got might not be the ones that did for the skipper."

"Can you prove that?"

"I can't," Shannon said. "You can, though. Quite easily."

"How?"

"I saw the surgeon remove the slugs and seal them in an envelope. Presumably he gave the envelope to O'Meara, who brought it to you. If it's on the level you should find the surgeon's prints on the envelope, right?"

Ziegler snapped his fingers. "It's a thought!" Then he paused. "Except, well, look, Shannon, those bullets had blood on them." He made a fretful mouth. "If Grady wasn't killed with them, then it's a damned cinch somebody was."

"Why, did you have the blood samples tested?"

"Tested? What do you mean?"

"To see whether it was human or animal. I wouldn't put it past O'Meara to run a caper, like shooting a dog or a cat with Duquesne's gun and then claiming the slugs were the ones that came from Grady's body."

"Now you're reaching," Ziegler said. "Anyhow I don't make bio-chemical tests. I'm ballistics, remember? How the hell would I know what kind of blood it was?"

"You wouldn't."

"All right, then. You want to order a biological?"

"No," Shannon said. He couldn't have, in any case. He no longer had the authority to order anything. "We'll take it for granted it was human blood."

"Whose?"

"I don't know that." His eyes were somber. "But we'll probably have a few more corpses turn up before this election is over. Maybe it will be one of them." He went to the door. "This will be about the last time I'll be able to contact you direct, Ziggy. I'm on the outside looking in, now. Anything you turn up you can pass on to Gus Vogel. Okay?"

"So they tied the can to you!"

"A whole goddamned string of cans," Shannon said bitterly. He patted Ziegler's shoulder. "Every time I move I sound like a guy trying to get through a barbwire entanglement. I had to see you just once, though, before I went into retirement."

"Yah. It's been nice knowing you."

"Well, goodnight, Ziggy." He went out and down to the street and caught a cab to his hotel. When he got up to his room, Floyd Duquesne was sitting on the edge of Shannon's bed. The gambler had a gun in his hand.

Duquesne's face and voice were expressionless. "Hello, Shannon." He did not get up.

"Well, I'll be God damned to hell!" Shannon said. "For Christ's sake what is this?"

Duquesne smiled thinly. "I escaped."

"Tell me something I don't already know."

"All right, I will," Duquesne smiled. "I escaped twice."

"That's swell. I'm very glad to meet you, Mr. Houdini. And if I seem not to understand what the hell you're talking about, put it down to my natural stupidity." Shannon didn't sound glad to meet anybody, but there was a sincere ring to his tone when he mentioned how stupid he was. He reached behind him with his good hand and snapped the lock on the door.

"A very good idea," Duquesne nodded approval.

Shannon went over to the dresser, got a bottle out of the lower drawer, found a glass and poured himself a generous drink. He sipped this meditatively, eyeing Duquesne. The gambler had managed to get some clothes somewhere, some of his own, apparently, because he looked his usual immaculate self. Shannon said, "There are lots of other places you could have escaped to besides this. I've already been accused of helping you."

Duquesne toyed with the gun. "I'm giving you credit for being a square copper, Shannon."

"Thanks a million, pal. Only you're wrong about the copper part. I'm not on the force any more. I'm just an indignant citizen."

"They broke you?"

Shannon inclined his head. "In pieces." He put his empty glass down, smacked his lips. And then, with a motion incredibly swift, his right hand buried itself in the slash pocket of his raglan, curled about the butt of his gun. "This makes us just about even, Duquesne. You've got a gun and I've got a gun. A Mexican stand-off. What do we do next?"

Duquesne said, "If I'd wanted to shoot you I would have done it long ago, wouldn't I?" He let the gun slide off his knee onto the floor.

Shannon flushed dully. "Yes, I guess you're right." He took his hand out of his pocket. "I guess I'm a little jittery tonight, not in the mood for games."

"Did you get hold of my brother?"

"Your what?"

"I'm just showing you that I trust you, Shannon. There aren't many people in the world that know. Ward Duffield, the eminent attorney, is my brother."

"The hell you say!"

Duquesne nodded. "A fact. We just happened to have somewhat different ideas about things when we were younger. I changed my name so I wouldn't embarrass him."

"You couldn't embarrass that guy," Shannon grunted, remembering the emotionless gray man with the club foot. "Why didn't he tell me?"

"In his spot, would you have?"

Shannon considered this. "Well, no, I guess I wouldn't have, at that. So you want to know where he is?"

"That's right."

"All right, I'll tell you. But you've got to tell me a few things first."

The gambler frowned. "Like what?"

"I find you here in my room with a nice fresh outfit of clothes and a gun in your hand. This doesn't exactly fit in with my theory that you were sprung by your enemies."

"I was, though."

"Well,damn it, what happened?"

"A couple of guys walked into the detention room. At first I thought they were dicks. Then one of them slugged the turnkey and I didn't think they were dicks any more. They walked me out under a pair of guns."

"Then what?" Shannon asked impatiently.

"Then I had a little good luck for a change," Duquesne admitted. "One of these punks was a reckless driver. He took a corner on two wheels and threw me against the other punk and I grabbed at his automatic and got it; a nice, stubby little gun, a .32 with an easy trigger." He looked at the weapon on the floor, reminiscently. "A very easy trigger. It was no job at all to squeeze it." He spread his hands, disparagingly.

"You shot both guys?"

Duquesne shrugged. "They were playing for keeps. Well, so was I."

Shannon drew a deep breath. "Just like that, hunh?"

"There was no other way."

"No, I suppose not. What happened then?"

"I got hold of a friend of mine and he rustled me some clothes. And as I say, I already had the gun. Of course I could have taken the other punk's rod, too; being dead he wouldn't need it any more. But I figured one was enough, so I didn't bother."

"Who were these guys you drilled?"

"I don't know. I didn't wait to find out." Gray eyes, very like his lame brother's, met Shannon's in a stare that told absolutely nothing. "Every cop in town is looking for me with orders to shoot on sight. A guy just doesn't stand around asking for it. I don't know who the guys were and that's that."

"All right, your brother is at the Corinthian."

Duquesne stood up. "Thank you, Shannon."

"I may want to see him myself, later on," Shannon said. "Meanwhile I want to know two more things, and don't give me any more of your I-don't-know routine. Where did you shoot these two mugs, and which one of the Third National tellers cashed that five-grand check for you?"

Duquesne, stooping, retrieved the fallen automatic. "The teller was a kid named Frank Little. The—ah—accident happened out on Gopher Flats, around Riverside and Terhune." He walked toward the door. "Anything else, Shannon?"

Shannon shook his head. "Not a thing, Floyd. Every detail of the whole setup is now as clear as mud. Maybe I'll be seeing you around, though."

"Maybe," Duquesne's voice was noncommittal.

"And if I find you've crossed me up it will be just too bad. Remember that, will you?"

"I'll keep it in mind," the gambler said. He went out.

Shannon waited until the sound of Duquesne's footsteps receded down the corridor. When he could no longer hear them he picked up the phone and called Precinct Five. "There was a shooting out your way an hour or so ago. Near Riverside and Terhune."

"What kind of a shooting?" the desk sergeant asked cautiously. You could tell he had been ribbed before.

"There's supposed to be a couple of dead hoods lying around out there somewhere. A guy just told me."

"He must have been kidding you, then. I ain't heard anything about it." There was a brief pause. Then: "Just a second. Car 17 is reporting in. Hold on." Another wait, longer this time. Presently came the sergeant's voice again. "You tell your pal he's all wet, fella. Seventeen ain't even saw a kid with a BB gun tonight. Crap!"

"Much obliged," Shannon said, and hung up.

He poured himself another drink, sipped it thoughtfully. Duquesne's lie seemed rather a pointless one. Why should he have come to Shannon with it in the first place?

Shannon sourly regarded his reflected image in the dresser mirror. "You're a sucker," he said. His reflection mocked him, saying: "You're a sucker." This seemed to make it unanimous.

It was quite a mess.

Duquesne was in it up to his ears. But how? Aside from the business of being taped for Grady's killing. How'd the five-grand check fit into the deal? Okay, Duquesne was competition for Lombardi and this was a cute way to get him into the lethal chamber. But why had the skipper's death been necessary? Why not just any Joe Doakes to be the meat in the trap?

Shannon sipped his drink again. How blind can a guy be? Grady had been killed because he was holding cards that would have ruined somebody. And the attempt on his own life via the bomb was because that certain somebody was afraid that Grady, being Shannon's friend, might have told him what he had. Simple enough. Even though Shannon didn't know a thing and the fear was just a pipe dream. That could work two ways: if he was going to be a target, somebody was bound to tip his mitt. Not that he was going to take any foolish chances. It behooved him to be very circumspect indeed in the immediate future.

Trying to determine the most circumspect thing to do, and still produce results, he began opening dresser drawers looking for a clean shirt. He found the shirt. He also found that someone had been messing around in his personal effects, though probably not in search of a shirt. Things had been put back carefully, a little too carefully, in fact. His mind went back to Duquesne. Had Floyd searched the room? Was this the real purpose of his visit, and the rest of it just a stall? Or had the searcher been someone else?

In either case Shannon derived a deal of satisfaction from the search itself. It proved that there was something tangible being sought, something you could get your fingers on. Ergo, Shannon had just as good a chance of finding it as anybody. He went to the phone and called Duffield at the Corinthian.

The attorney's voice was inflectionless. "Yes, Shannon?"

"Look," Shannon said, "a certain guy who said he was your brother left her a while ago. I understood he was going to see you. Is he there?"

There was a little wait. Duffield's tone, when he spoke, was uncharacteristically harsh. "I don't know what you are talking about."

Shannon cursed without warmth. "Goddam it to hell, would he have told me what he did if I wasn't to be trusted? You lawyers make me sick at my stomach. So look, whether you admit it or not, this brother of yours was here and gave me a song and dance about killing a couple of mugs that have since disappeared. He's on the loose. If I were in his shoes I'd probably be hunting for the guy that framed me. You'd better stop him."

Duffield didn't say anything.

There was a knock on the door and Shannon, carefully placing the phone on its side, went to the door and unlocked it. Two dicks from the homicide squad pushed in. One was a very tough hombre named Costigan. He had been up on charges two or three times for shooting first and asking questions afterward. The other guy was a small, rat-faced man whose only reason for being on the police force was that he was Captain O'Meara's brother-in-law.

Shannon was very careful about keeping his hand away from his overcoat pocket. "Hello, lice."

"The chief wants to see you," Costigan said.

"Regan? He hasn't left town yet?"

"Long ago. The chief that wants to see you is Chief O'Meara."

"What about?"

"Floyd Duquesne was seen leaving this hotel a few minutes ago. O'Meara thinks you might know where he is. Let's go."

CHAPTER FOUR

SHANNON RAISED HIS VOICE. "Now just a minute! How in the hell should I know where Duquesne is? You guys have got a lot of crust, even for cops. Of all the—"

"I said let's go," Costigan rasped.

Shannon balked. "This is a public hotel, isn't it? And if you saw Duquesne leaving it why didn't you pick him up?"

The rat-faced dick said, "We didn't see him. It was some other guy and he didn't know who it was until it was too late. So then he called in and we come on over." His scanty jaw made an effort to jut truculently, but it was a pretty feeble attempt. "You son of a bitch, who are you to be asking for explanations? If you want to argue about it we'll give you all the argument you can hold up under. And then some." He got a sap out of his pocket, very ostentatiously. Costigan took out a gun.

Shannon backed toward the table, screening the phone. "Is this a pinch?"

"Maybe," the rat-faced dick said.

Costigan said, "And then again, maybe not. O'Meara wants a little talk with you."

"O'Meara probably wants to beat the hell out of me."

"We could save him the trouble," Costigan suggested.

Rat-face leered. "It would be a pleasure, pal."

"I don't doubt it," Shannon said. Then: "All right, put away your persuaders. I'll go down with you."

"Now that's what I call being sensible."

"Can I call my attorney?"

"No," Costigan said.

The rat-faced dick laughed raucously. "You won't need no mouthpiece to do your talking for you, you bastard. You'll do it all by yourself. With or without your front teeth," he added, "depending on whether you say the right words."

Shannon let his shoulders droop in resignation. Rat-face sidled up and took the gun out of Shannon's pocket. The three of them then left the room, went down in the elevator, got into the squad car and drove to headquarters. It was well along in the small hours of the morning.

Night janitors were busy swabbing down the long marble halls. A telegraph key clicked fitfully in the Communications Bureau, but there weren't many people around. Most of the ground-glass office doors were dark, the graveyard shift either out on the streets or asleep.

Captain O'Meara was alone in his office. His olive face looked haggard and there were dark pouches under his eyes from lack of sleep. Costigan closed and locked the door. Then he lifted a fist and smacked Shannon in the mouth. Shannon sat down hard in the chair which Rat-face had thoughtfully placed behind him. Nobody said anything for a full minute.

Then O'Meara looked at Costigan. "He give you any trouble?"

"Unh-unh."

"You frisk him?"

"We got his gun, is all."

Rat-face said, "Like candy from a baby."

"A one-armed baby," Shannon said. "I never saw such a brave pair of coppers."

This time it was Rat-face who hit him in the mouth. The guy didn't pack the wallop that Costigan packed though.

Shannon, with his one free hand, wiped a little blood off his lips. His eyes were red hot. He turned them on O'Meara. "I thought you wanted to see me about Duquesne."

"That's right," O'Meara said.

"Well, you're seeing me. When do you trot out the lengths of rubber hose?"

"I believe the boys can do well enough with their fists," the acting-chief said. "In the meantime you don't mind if they turn out your pockets, do you?"

"Would it do me any good if I objected?"

"Not a bit." O'Meara gestured to the two dicks.

Rat-face and Costigan did everything but rip Shannon's clothes off him without finding anything that O'Meara seemed to want. They were not particularly careful of his broken arm. Little rivulets of sweat ran down off his forehead when they had finished with him, and the nostrils of his big nose flared, like a horse's after a hard run. He hadn't lifted a hand, though. They couldn't say afterward that he had put up a fight.

O'Meara leaned back in his swivel chair. It creaked complainingly under his weight. "Now then, Shannon, where is Duquesne?"

"I don't know."

"I'll ask you one more time. Just one. Lie to me again and you won't enjoy what happens to you. Where is Duquesne?"

"I don't know."

Costigan took a sap out of one of the desk drawers, hefting it. Somebody knocked on the door.

O'Meara flicked a worried glance toward the hall and motioned for Costigan to put the sap away. "See who it is, Charlie," he told his brother-in-law. Then, as Rat-face started to obey: "No, wait a minute." He jerked his head at a communicating door leading into an inner office. Rat-face and Costigan closed in on Shannon.

Shannon yelled, "In here, Duffield!"

The glass door shook under a series of blows that threatened to smash in its frosted panel. O'Meara shrugged. "Okay, open up and let him in."

Costigan went over and unlocked the door. Ward Duffield walked in, limping on his club foot. He had Runyon of the *Telegram* with him. He was quite a guy, Duffield. Shannon guessed that there weren't many tricks in the bag this gray-faced, gray-haired lawyer hadn't memorized.

Duffield looked at O'Meara. "Warrant?"

O'Meara's eyes had a harried expression. "Now see here, counsellor, what's your interest in this thing?"

"I understood that Mr. Shannon had been arrested."

O'Meara glared savagely at Costigan and his brother-in-law. You knew that he couldn't figure it out and neither could they. Shannon thought it unnecessary to tell them that he had been talking to Duffield on the telephone from his hotel room and had deliberately left he line open.

Duffield apparently didn't believe in wasting words. He said again, "Warrant?"

O'Meara had to admit he didn't have one. "This wasn't a pinch, counsellor."

"No? What was it?"

"We just wanted to have a talk with Shannon about a certain matter."

"What?"

"Well, another client of yours was seen leaving Shannon's hotel, and—"

"Was he seen in Shannon's company?"

"No."

With a slender forefinger, Duffield stirred the little pile of Shannon's personal belongings. "No doubt you thought that Mr. Shannon had my other client in his pocket?"

Jack Runyon was looking at Shannon's bruised lip. "You run into a door, keed?"

"All right!" O'Meara stood up suddenly, thrusting his chair back so hard that it crashed into the far wall.

"God damn it to hell!" He pointed a shaking finger at Shannon. "But you watch your step, you shanty-Irish bastard!"

"You called me that once before. I didn't like it then and I don't like it now."

"The hell with what you like or don't like. One more caper out of you and we'll nail you to the cross, understand?" He looked at Duffield. "You're playing with dynamite, counsellor."

Shannon's mouth quirked in a mirthless grin as he heard this phrase. It was getting a little shopworn, he reflected. Duffield looked at Shannon's broken arm. "Dynamite has its uses." He gave Jack Runyon a significant glance. "Its uses are not always pleasant, would you say? If you get the connection."

"I see what you mean," Runyon sounded awed.

The attorney smiled at him. "Better luck and a better story for your paper next time, my young friend." He took Shannon's elbow and they went out and down to the street.

There was a taxi waiting. In it, heading down Broadway. Shannon said, "Thanks, Duffield."

"That's all right." The gray man smiled sardonically. "You're smarter than I gave you credit for, Shannon. You knew I'd come, didn't you?"

"Because I knew he was your brother?"

"Because he *is* my brother. There's a little distinction there. If Floyd thought enough of you to tell you that, then you must be all right. In spite of his faults, Floyd knows men. I respect his judgment. You counted on that."

Shannon said, "Well, sure. But don't get the idea that I was putting the pressure on you because I knew about the relationship." He scowled. "I had no intention of telling it to O'Meara whether you showed up or not."

"That never entered my mind," Duffield said. "It wasn't fear of what you might spill that brought me downtown. I came because you've shot square with Floyd thus far."

"And I'll go on shooting square with him as long as he shoots square with me, Shannon said. He paused. "Have you seen him?"

"Not yet. I left word at the hotel that I would be back shortly. He may be waiting even now."

Shannon looked out the cab's rear window. His eyes got narrow. "We're being tailed."

"Of course. O'Meara isn't exactly a fool."

The gray man's face set in grim lines. You knew he realized the kind of game they were playing, and that he knew the stakes were high.

"I'll drop off at the next corner," Shannon said. "One tail can't follow both of us if we separate."

"Good enough."

Shannon went on, "Unless Floyd was lying to me, he doesn't know who jacked him out of the can. On the other hand, maybe he does know. Find out if you can, Duffield. I'll contact you later in the morning."

"Very well."

Shannon leaned forward, tapped on the glass. "Take the next turn fast, fella, then brake it a second till I fall off."

The cabby nodded, romped down on his throttle and twisted his wheel to the right at the next intersection, then hit his brakes hard. Shannon opened the door as rubber screamed. He jumped and landed running, he asphalt stinging his soles, and then sprawled into the protecting shelter of a darkened store entry.

The cab gathered speed again. It vanished around the far corner. So did the prowl car following it.

Panting, Shannon pulled himself up and stood for a moment in the deep shadows, his face puckered with thought. There was nothing more for him to do right now, he decided, except just to lie low; to elude surveillance either by the cops or anyone else.

He walked three blocks to an all night drug store, bought two packs of cigarettes, walked another block to a small second-rate hotel across from his own and asked for a room on the fourth floor. Presently he was sitting at a window which commanded a good view of the deserted street, the entrance to his own hotel opposite and even one of the windows of his own room. He had an idea that somebody might come looking for him again.

Before anyone did, though, Shannon went to sleep.

The sun shining in his eyes brought Shannon up with a start. Painfully he stood up, yawning widely, and slogged back and forth across the room half a dozen times to loosen his muscles. He discovered that his broken arm not only ached like an abscessed tooth, it itched; and he couldn't scratch it because of the ton of plaster they had hung on him. The weight of this, having been suspended in the sling draped around his neck all night, had given his head a sort of compensatory cant to starboard; and his neck-sinews protested painfully when he made a correcting adjustment. His eyes felt as if they had recently been laved with glue.

All told, he was in no very cheerful mood when he checked out of his fleabag, crossed the street to the hotel where he lived and went upstairs to his own room. "Well, for Christ's sake!" he said. Somebody had ransacked the room thoroughly this time. It looked as though the wrecking crew had moved in and made permanent camp. Shannon stood in the middle of the mess, cursing big round Irish oaths that seemed to roll up out of his chest without the slightest effort on his part.

He struggled dismally through an inadequate bath and shave and got into some clean clothes. The shirt was the worst. He had to get his broken arm into the sleeve of that, which was like trying to insert the trunk of a redwood tree down a gopher hole. He finally tore off the sleeve at the shoulder and threw it out the window. "The hell with it," he snarled.

His tie gave him less difficulty; it was already looped and knotted from a previous wearing, so by a little jockeying he was able to get it up where it belonged. He let his coat sleeve dangle, readjusted the sling which the emergency hospital guys had given him and hanging his useless arm across his chest. The gun he had gotten back from Costigan and O'Meara he thrust into the waistband of his trousers, first making certain that it was fully loaded in case of need.

He went down to breakfast.

The waitress was a big-hipped blonde who looked as if she had been around. Her name was Florrie and she chewed gum. She fetched Shannon the morning papers.

Shannon opened a paper. Floyd Duquesne's escape had the headlines, of course. It was a foregone conclusion that his disappearance, added to the evidence already in the possession of the police, establishing the gambler's guilt beyond the shadow of a doubt. Acting-Chief George O'Meara came in for a bit of censure for having permitted the murderer of Captain Grady to escape, but he had promised an early arrest. The turnkey was in the hospital and was expected to recover.

Mayor Argyle: *"It is unfortunate."*

Shannon almost choked on that one. Argyle certainly wasn't saying anything that could be held against him in the forthcoming election. Shannon wondered if His Honor had finally capitulated to Big Nick Lombardi and promised to be a good boy in the future.

District Attorney Jorgensen: *"Captain O'Meara, in my considered opinion, is not to be blamed. Handicapped as he is by the inexplicable absence of Chief Regan, who returned to his desk only long enough to issue an official statement and who then again flew north to attend a convention of peace officers, leaving this entire sorry scandal in O'Meara's lap, it is little wonder that O'Meara is confronted by difficulties. Coupled with the obvious dissension and internal strife within the police department, the escape of a prisoner being held on suspicion of murder is not at all surprising. My office is making an immediate investigation of the rumor that a former lieutenant of detectives was implicated in the escape.*

Shannon sipped his orange juice. It tasted sour, or possibly it was Jorgensen's pyrotechnical rhetoric that put the sour taste in his mouth. Every time Jorgensen got a chance to be quoted in print he mangled the English language the way Florrie did oranges, extracting the last ultimate ounce of juice along with a great deal of pulp and considerable bitter oil from the peel. Shannon scowled and turned to the second page, where there was about a stick and a half covering the car explosion in the police garage and a boxed editorial concerning this.

"Subsequent occurrences," the editorial said, *"make it a moot question whether the attack was meant to do any actual damage, or was merely an attempt to make a presumed hero out of an officer known to be a friend of the deceased Captain Grady, whose demise, by the way, was tinctured by a distinct aura of graft, bribery and corruption in high places. It is to be noted, in passing, that the officer under discussion escaped with*

merely a broken arm, and later is known to have consorted with the missing Floyd Duquesne as well as with Duquesne's legal counsel, the noted criminal attorney, Ward Duffield.

Shannon, eating bacon and buckwheat cakes, concluded that the editorial writer must have studied English in the same correspondence school class with District Attorney Jorgensen. Their styles were as identical as two of the ornamental holes on a four-holer Buick—and as showy as the fish-tail rear fenders on a Cadillac. Carrying the metaphor to its logical conclusion, Shannon decided that the pompous utterances of both the district attorney and the editorialist carried about as much substance as the vapors from a Chevrolet's exhaust pipe.

Acting-Chief George O'Meara: *"There is nothing of personal animosity in my suspension of Lieutenant Shannon. I simply feel that I must have the utmost cooperation at this time from every member of the department in order to do the job I have to do."*

Shannon gulped his coffee.

There were a lot of words here, no doubt calculated to explain something, but as far as Shannon could see nothing was explained. The stage was set, though. The public was all agog for further developments and the side that furnished the biggest explosion would probably win the election. The trouble was, Shannon didn't seem to be on anybody's side. He thought about going to see the opposition candidate for mayor, decided against that for the present in favor of calling on Frank Little, the Third National bank teller who had cashed a five thousand dollar bearer check for Floyd Duquesne.

Having reached this decision and finished his breakfast simultaneously, Shannon paid his check, left a quarter tip for Florrie and went out.

There was quite a crowd at the bank. Shannon looked down the long line of tellers' cages without seeing anybody even remotely resembling Frank Little's description. Finally he walked over to the marble rail enclosing the officers' desks and spoke to an assistant cashier whose embossed brass name plate had *Robert B. Leslie* on it in letters polished to a burnished glow. The guy was a middle-aged man with slightly wavy hair, a thickening middle and a mustache of which he seemed inordinately vain. He wore gold-rimmed glasses but his blue eyes looked as if they didn't need them. "Something?" he said politely.

"I'd like to see Frank Little."

"Mr. Little isn't here this morning."

Shannon looked at the wall clock. It was after eleven. "He's supposed to be on duty, isn't he?"

"He's probably sick. He hasn't been at all well lately. What was it you wanted to see him about?"

"His health." Shannon reached in his pocket for his badge and remembered that he didn't have one any more. He manufactured a smile. "I seem to have mislaid his home address. Could you let me have it, please?"

The cashier referred to a card index with an easy show of efficiency, then picked up a ball point pen to scribble on a sheet of memo paper. The pen refused at first to track ink, then it blurted a blue, gooey gob onto the paper. Robert B. Leslie snatched off his spectacles, said, "Damn these things!" under his breath, hurled paper and pen into a nearby waste-basket, replaced the glasses and picked up a pencil. He wrote something down and handed it to Shannon. "I hope you find Mr. Little feeling better," he said. His voice was pious but his eyes had an infuriated glitter, and his handwriting bore the crabbed shakiness of a man who is sorely tried.

Shannon thanked him, turned hastily away and ran smack into Frances McGowan, looking very smart in tailored tweeds. Fran gave him a bright nod. "Hello, darling."

Shannon eyed her dourly. "What do you want?"

"A little peace of mind," she said, no longer bright and cheerful. "You're worrying me sick, John J. Shannon."

The cashier stiffened at his resk behind the marble railing. "For God's sake, are you the Lieutenant Shannon who was blown up by a pineapple?"

"It was a grapefruit," Shannon said peevishly, and regarded Fran with a scowl of resentment. "You're certainly a big help. It isn't enough that I've got a busted arm to identify me. You have to come around shouting my name all over the place. Why don't you get a megaphone?"

"Well, if you won't stay in your room where you belong, so people can find you—"

"How did you know I'd be here?"

"You told me."

Shannon vehemently denied this, calling on God to witness that he had done no such thing.

"You did too," Fran said. "You told me you were going to work on—"

Shannon seized her arm, suppressing a desire to shake her. "If you don't shut up you're going to have to see your dentist about some new front teeth." He lifted his voice for the benefit of the cashier. "Come on, pet, let's have a soda."

Gus Vogel came rolling across the lobby on his short, thick legs. He doffed his green-black derby out of deference to Frances. "Is something the matter, John J.?"

Looking like a guy on the verge of a stroke, Shannon breathed, "You, too? Christ, this must be my lucky day. I've hit the jackpot."

"Well," Gus said apologetically, "I've been trying all night to find you. Then I remembered you said something about working on the check angle, so I came here."

Shannon stared wonderingly from one to the other. "You mean you didn't come together?"

"Certainly not!" Frances said. "I'm a rugged individualist." She smiled nicely at Vogel's round infantile face. "Gus is a rugged individualist too, aren't you, Gus?"

Gus mopped sweat from his forehead. "Sure, Miss McGowan, sure. Anything you say." He put worried eyes on Shannon's darkly scowling face. "I had to get to you, John J., before you cut any more capers about things that ain't so."

"Meaning exactly what?"

"Them slugs they dug out of the skipper," Vogel said. "There ain't no doubt now where they came from. They really came out of Floyd Duquesne's gun."

Shannon didn't say anything for a minute. He just stood there like a punch-drunk fighter. He had been so sure of the switch that he would have bet his life on it.

Presently he snarled, "Ziegler, in Ballistics, tell you this, or did you get it from a gypsy fortune teller?"

"It was Ziggy," Vogel nodded. "He told me what you were trying to prove, only it turned out it wasn't so."

"How did he pin it down?"

"The surgeon's prints was on the envelope. You saw the slugs taken out and put in that same envelope. The slugs matched up with Duquesne's gun."

"I see."

"I guess that settles it, hunh, John J.?"

"Yes," Shannon said wearily. His face had harsh lines, deeply etched from nostrils to mouth corners, and his eyes seemed suddenly sunken in his head. "Yes, that settled it, all right." He took off his hat, ran a sleeve across his forehead. "Well, the Shannons have guessed wrong before."

"Not this Shannon," Vogel said. "This is the first time I ever saw you figure something the wrong way."

"Stop buttering me," Shannon rasped. "I've made my mistakes and I'll go on making them. This one just makes it a little harder, is all. It means somebody stole Duquesne's gun and used that on Grady instead of the way I had it doped out. O'Meara was honest about that anyway."

Frances dropped her air of half-witted nonchalance. "It means more than that, Shan. It means you let a screwy idea get you tossed out of the department. If you hadn't practically accused O'Meara—"

He looked at her, "All right, it's done, isn't it? You want me to go and apologize to him?"

"It mightn't be a bad idea."

"I'll wait until I talk to Chief Regan."

Vogel said, "I already tried to do that."

"The hell you did!"

"Well, I tried to. I didn't get to, though. I phoned up at his hotel up in San Francisco but he had went out and wasn't expected back until after he finished making his speech at the convention. A morning-session speech," Vogel added in an aggrieved tone. "You might think a chief from a city as important as this one would anyhow get an afternoon spot on the program, not in the morning when probably half the guys in the audience has got hangovers and won't pay no attention to him."

"God damn it, stick to the point!" Shannon's exasperation was rapidly stretching past the limit of endurance. "You called Regan long distance. Why?"

Vogel got a hurt look. "Why? Because I thought he ought to know about the murder slugs matching Duquesne's gun, and about somebody saying they seen Duquesne coming out of your hotel, and you being canned off the force by O'Meara on account of it. Also about Duffield keeping you from getting pinched, and—"

"That's fine. While you're at it maybe you'd like to tell him my room was ransacked some time between five o'clock this morning and ten. That's the only part he doesn't already know if he's looked at the newspaper reports."

Gus shifted on his feet, embarrassed. "I never claimed to have no brains, John J.," he said mildly. "If you want to know what I really phoned the chief about, it was to try and persuade him to come on home and take over his desk and give you back your badge so you'd be on the force again. That's just exactly what I would of said to him, too, only I couldn't reach him."

"All right. I'm sorry," Shannon growled. He patted Vogel awkwardly on the shoulder. Then he yelled, "Only from now on I'll thank you to keep your fat nose out of my business! Who the hell said I wanted my badge back? I wouldn't have the job if they plated it with gold and presented it to me on a uranium platter. All I want is the bastard that killed the skipper. I intend to get him—and I don't have to be a lousy cop to do it!"

Shannon suddenly remembered something. He faced Vogel. "Look, Gus, there ought to be a couple of stiffs lying around town some place. You hear anything about it?"

Vogel sucked in his lips. "Jesus!" He was not ordinarily a profane guy, so it was patent that he was suffering a profound emotional disturbance. "Did you do that, John J.?"

"Did I do what?" Shannon glared at him.

"There was a couple guys ran their car off a pier down at the beach some time last night, only I think they were shot first. In fact, I'm pretty sure they were. The holes in their heads didn't look like the fish had chewed them. I never heard of no fish making like a bullet hole."

"Who were they?"

"Who were who?"

"The guys with the holes in their heads!" Shannon yelled.

"Don't you know?"

Shannon turned purple. "One of these days, Gus—" He held himself with a mighty effort. "No, I don't know. Would I be asking if I did?"

"Well, you knew they were dead, didn't you? And it ain't been in the papers yet." Vogel, obviously, was torn between his loyalty to Shannon and his training as a cop. Frances looked at Shannon as if she expected to see the blood still on his hands. He controlled himself, although anybody could see that he did this with considerable difficulty.

"Look, the both of you," he said. "I didn't kill those guys. I happened to hear about them, never mind how, but I don't know who they were. So now, granting that I deserve the benefit of the doubt, would you mind telling me before I blow my goddamned top?"

"They were out-of-town talent, Vogel said. "We placed them as from St. Louis. Now what do you suppose they was doing here?"

"Getting themselves shot in the head," Shannon said ungraciously. He put on his hat. "Well, it certainly has been nice meeting you folks." He made a sarcastic mouth. "Don't think it hasn't been pleasant, because it hasn't."

"Now, John J.—"

"Goodbye, please."

Frances looked at Vogel. "Run along, Gussie, there's a good boy."

"You run along too," Shannon said. "There's a good girl. I've got work to do." He started for the door.

Frances hung onto his arm. "Whither thou goest."

"Now cut that out."

She turned to Vogel. "Haven't you gone yet, Gus? Funny, but I thought you were leaving us."

"Well, sure," he said. "Sure, only—"

"Never mind, just run along."

He looked miserably at Shannon. "I guess maybe I ain't wanted, hunh?"

"Sure you're wanted. Somewhere else," Shannon said. "Take Miss McGowan with you. Get lost."

Fran said, "Not this time, Gussie. You'll have to get lost by yourself. Do you mind awfully?"

Vogel finally took off his derby, peered into it without finding any inspiration, sighed, put the derby on and blinked at Frances. "I suppose you want to talk to John J. alone, Miss McGowan."

"Now what could have given you that idea?" she smiled sweetly. The smile took the sting out of it.

Vogel eyed her, doubtfully. "Well—"

She leaned down and kissed him lightly on the cheek. "We'll be seeing you." Vogel, blushing, waddled out of the bank. Fran turned to Shannon. "Now what do we do, darling?"

"I hear a band," Shannon said. "Let's go out and watch the parade." They went out to the street, and sure enough there was a band, and a parade, and at least eighty thousand potential voters looking at it. Mayor Paul Shacklewood Argyle had taken advantage of his position and was using the fire department to help get him elected for another term. The voters seemed to see nothing especially ludicrous in uniformed city employees carrying election banners. Shannon wondered why Argyle had not pressed the street cleaners and sewage departments into the ranks of marchers. He thought that they would have been more appropriate than the firemen.

CHAPTER FIVE

THE HOUSE WAS ONE OF THOSE you find by the score in the Westlake district. Carefully preserved, dignified in their age, they remind you of the dowager-and-lorgnette period. Jap gardners take care of their lawns by contract; the cars you see parked on the streets and the people you see issuing from the houses are definitely middle class, but an indefinable air of polite opulence still clings. You remember that Mrs. Astorbilt once lived here, and the school teachers and the better-paid clerks who live here now—*Sunny corner room in private home for rent*—usually comport themselves as though she still lived here.

Shannon hadn't been able to get rid of Frances McGowan short of knocking her cold. They got out of the cab together, mounted the porch together. Shannon rang the bell. Presently a trim Negro maid in stiffly starched dress and apron opened the door. "Yes, sir?" She had no accent whatever

Shannon said, "Does Mr. Frank Little live here?"

"Yes, sir."

"I'd like to see him."

"I don't know if he's at home, sir."

"Well, you could find out, couldn't you?"

The girl hesitated. She looked a little distressed. Her brown eyes shifted uneasily. A regal, white-haired woman who could have posed for Madame Pompadour appeared at the farther extremity of the long hall. "Who is it, Martha?"

The maid turned to her. "A gentleman says he wants to see Mr. Frank, Mrs. Little."

The white-haired woman came forward. "How do you do?"

"Hello," Shannon said. This was going to be more difficult than he had figured. He hadn't counted on Frank Little having a mother. He took off his hat. "They said at the bank that Frank hadn't come down this morning. Is he at home?"

Mrs. Little's eyes showed a trace of fright. It went away when she looked at Frances. Mrs. Little was reassured. "Won't you come in?"

They went in, followed the maid into a small parlor. The white-haired woman disappeared up carpeted stairs. Presently she came down again. She was definitely worried now. "Frank isn't in," she said. She looked at the maid. "Martha, did you make up his room this morning?"

"No, ma'am, not yet."

Mrs. Little's hands made a swift fluttery movement, as swiftly stilled. "But—but surely he must have been home last night!" she said. "He never stays out all night." She saw the maid looking at her and her cheeks grew slightly pink. "Well, almost never. At least he usually lets me know—"

"Are you trying to tell us his bed hasn't been slept in?" Shannon asked her.

"I don't know. It's made."

Martha said, "And I didn't make it. Not this morning."

"Of course," Frank Little's mother said, "he might have left early this morning and made the bed up himself before he went out. Although why he would do a thing like that when he knows Martha's job is to—"

"Mrs. Little," Shannon said gently, and eased his left arm into a more comforable position, "could we take a look at his room, please?"

"Why—why, wh-what on earth for?"

Shannon tried to be easy with her. "I don't want to worry you, Mrs. Little, but I think I'd better tell you I'm from the police."

"The police?" Her hand went to her throat. "Is—You don't—I mean—You don't think anything's happened to him, do you?"

"Of course not," Shannon assured her. "In spite of what you said a minute ago, Frank does stay out all night, doesn't he? Especially in recent weeks, or maybe recent months?"

"Well—yes. Rather often. That is, too often for my peace of mind. But—"

"There, you see? It's nothing at all for you to bother about. All this worrying you're doing is for nothing. We're just checking up on a guy your son knew."

"Oh, I—I see."

"Perhaps if we could look at his room," Shannon said.

They went upstairs. It was a man's room; a man who, in a limited fashion, was a sybarite. There was a fireplace, and on the old fashioned marble mantel were three or four cabinet photographs of girls who, if Shannon was any judge, wouldn't be satisfied with a bank clerk's salary. Mrs. Little indicated a hand-tinted eight-by-ten in a glass easel. "This is my son."

He was a good looking kid, somewhere in his late twenties at a guess. The mouth was a little weak but the eyes looked at you straight enough. Shannon went over to a littered desk. Somebody had been doing a lot of feverish figuring lately. In the wastebasket by the desk Shannon found a couple of torn-up checks. They had been made out to a guy namel Tex Boyer.

Shannon happened to know that Boyer fronted a horse parlor and gambling layout for Big Nick Lombardi. At least one of his ideas seemed to be working out. He looked at Mrs. Little. "Well—uh—I guess there's nothing here, ma'am. Sorry to have troubled you. A cop has to follow all his leads, though, no matter how crazy they may seem."

She put a hand on his arm, looked deep into his eyes. "You're lying, aren't you?"

"Who, me?"

"There *is* something wrong with Frank."

He glanced helplessly at Frances, found no succor there, and finally straightened his shoulders, did his best to sound convincing. "Honestly, I don't think there's a thing wrong, Mrs. Little. Like I told you, we just thought maybe we could get a line on this other guy through your son."

"Well, I'll tell Frank you were here."

"Do that," Shannon said cordially. "The name is Wilberforce, Sergeant Wilberforce." He grabbed Fran's arm and practically ran down the stairs.

Outside, in the taxi, he let out a great whooshing breath and mopped his forehead with his sleeve. "Whew! That was a tough one, kitten."

"Old hardboiled Shannon," Frances said. She made a very inelegant sound with her mouth, but her eyes were shining. After a while she said, "How did you guess the kid had been staying out nights?"

"It figured. Dames."

"How did you know that while you were still in the parlor?" she demanded. "You hadn't been upstairs yet. You hadn't seen the pictures on his mantel." She added, "They looked like tramps to me. Didn't they to you?"

"Oh, I don't know." Then, when she froze, he said, "Sure, hon. But definitely tramps. That's what I meant when I said it figured. It would take dames like that to make the kid do what he did."

"Don't explain that. Let me puzzle it out for myself." Frances sounded a little nettled.

Shannon shrugged irritably. "Help yourself. While you're doing it I wish to God I could find the punk. Somehow, though, I don't think I will. I don't think anybody will."

"I don't get it," Frances said.

"You will," he promised. "You'll get it in the neck if you keep tagging around after me. I got fooled on the slugs, maybe, but this check business is adding up."

"To what?"

"By the look of the kid, and the dames he's been running around with, I'd say he probably needed more money than he was making. A bank teller's pay isn't a king's ransom by a hell of a distance." Shannon scowled thoughtfully. "He needed more dough, and, trying to get it, he got hooked by this Tex Boyer louse. Maybe he even dipped into the bank for a few bucks."

"Boyer?"

Shannon explained about the torn-up checks he had found in the wastebasket, and about Boyer running one of Nick Lombardi's joints. "Either Boyer, or Nick Lombardi, through Boyer, put the squeeze on Little. Say the kid really had let some bank money stick to his fingers; with that as leverage it would have been easy for Lombardi to force him into a corner, coerce him into substituting cash for Floyd Duquesne's five-grand check. Now do you get it?"

"I'm beginning to."

"This would keep the bank's records straight," Shannon continued, "and at the same time give Lombardi a Duquesne check that wasn't canceled. I knew it would have to be worked through a teller, because it's the teller who rubber-stamps the checks as he takes them in; at least when he totals up at the end of the day. He paid out the five thousand dollars to Duquesne for the check. Later he replaced that amount of cash in his till, the cash having been given him by Lombardi, or Boyer. His books were then in balance with his cash and he could hand the check to Boyer to give to Lombardi. Simple enough?"

"Oh, very. And so?"

Shannon's lips moved soundlessly for a moment. Then: "If that was how it happened, would they let the punk keep on running around after he pulled the trick for them and gave them the check? He was a weak sister or he wouldn't have done the job in the first place. So there was a good chance that he'd crack sometime. Let's go back to our assumption that he was short in his accounts. Say Boyer or Lombardi had promised him enough money to make up his shortages if he would work the check trick. Then say they deliberately neglected to keep their end of the bargain. Now, suppose Little disappears. If he doesn't show up it will be assumed he just took a powder because his accounts were short. The bank examiners will go over his books with a fine comb. The audit will prove he was a thief. His disappearance will confirm this. The Bankers' Protective outfit, the bonding company and the police will search all over hell for him. Do you think they'll ever find him—alive?"

Frances shivered a little. "I think I'm scared, Shan."

"That makes two of us," he said sourly.

They rode back downtown to the Third National. Shannon, getting out, said, "You wait here, hon. I just want to make sure the kid hasn't showed." He pushed through the bank's big revolving door, crossed the lobby to the assistant cashier's desk. Frank Little was still absent. Shannon, chuckling a little at his own cleverness, chose a side-street exit instead of the main one, went outdoors and climbed into a cab of his own. Miss Frances McGowan would have a nice long wait.

The hacker kept peering at Shannon in the rear vision mirror. Finally he screwed half around in his seat. "Ain't your name Shannon?"

"That's right."

"I been reading the papers. You ain't a dick no more."

"That's right, too."

"I see you got a broken arm," the guy remarked in a conversational tone.

Shannon, trying to think, was becoming annoyed. "Say, what is this, an I.Q. test?"

"I was just figuring," the guy said, "that now would be a hell of a swell time to give you a goddamned good bust in the nose and not run no chanst of getting busted back."

Shannon really looked at the hacker this time. "What for?"

"On account of you pinched me once."

"The hell I did!"

"For something that wasn't none of your lousy business, too," the guy sounded pretty bitter about it. "After all, she was *my* wife." He seemed to be mulling this over in his mind for a minute. Then he swung into an alley and braked the cab to a halt. "Yep," he announced. "Now would be just about the right time." He opened the rear door. "Out, buster."

"You wouldn't pick on a cripple, would you?"

"I would and I'm gonna. Get out. I don't want no blood dirtying up the upholstery."

Shannon, scarcely moving from his seat, kicked the hacker in the stomach. As the guy turned green and doubled over, Shannon reached out and got a handful of shirt, necktie and uniform collar. He hauled in slack, butted the cabby between the eyes and then held him, until his, Shannon's, big nose almost touched the bulbous one belonging to the hacker. The guy's eyes were slightly crossed and he looked unwell. Shannon said, "Listen, scum, without a badge and with only one arm I'm still a better man that you are. Believe it?"

The guy said he did. He protested that he believed it very much indeed. In a voice thickened by what seemed to be sinus trouble, but which might have been the result of the butting Shannon had given him, he proclaimed that he was a dumb son of a bitch to have ever thought otherwise.

"Then get in and drive," Shannon said. He leaned back in his seat and resumed his thinking. Four or five more blocks brought them down on Spring, opposite the financial center. "Stop here," Shannon said. The driver obeyed, got out and opened the door for him. Shannon looked at the meter.

The hacker said, "Never mind, this is on me. I always thought the other time was a phony, an accident, sort of, but I see I was wrong. You should of beat the crud outa me."

Shannon examined the guy's license. "Well, this is very nice of you, Mr. Osterwicz. I'll remember you in case I need a hacker again." He crossed the street in a middle-of-the-block pedestrian zone, holding up four lanes of traffic as if he owned the town.

The ticker club had originally been a private affair, limited to members of the stock exchange. When things got so tough that brokers could no longer pay their dues the board of regents had let down the bars, admitting even lawyers ond bankers. In those days the lawyers and bankers weren't doing so well either. Finally the mortgage holders closed the place up, recovered what they could under a forced sale, and the new owner turned out to be Big Nick Lombardi.

Everybody had thought this was a laugh on Lombardi. He fooled them and made the place into a mint.

The brokers still ate there. So did the bankers and the lawyers. Their clerks patronized the club so that they could feel as important as their bosses. Upstairs, the games ran day and night, on the theory that when you got tired of losing money in the market you could relax by dropping a few dollars on the horses, or at the crap tables. The cops had never been able to prove that the games were there because by the time the cops arrived the games had vanished. There were some who claimed that this was not pure legerdemain; they said that Tex Boyer, the lessee, was wired into Headquarters. Tex himself never confirmed or denied this. He just went on making money for Nick Lombardi.

Shannon pushed through the noonday crush at the bar, caught an elevator to the second floor. This was the tea room. Ladies were admitted. Shannon took his hat off in deference to the ladies, denied the headwaiter the privilege of showing him to a table, moved easily across the big gold-and-pastel-decorated room, came to Tex Boyer's door and knocked on it.

"Come on in, Shannon," somebody called.

Shannon thought this was very funny. He thought it was a cute trick no matter how it was done. It probably made a tremendous impression on visiting firemen, it was a swell way to duck process servers. He opened the door and went in.

The office was not quite spacious enough for a hockey game but it would have made a pretty good ballroom. The ceiling was high and had fumed oak beams, the walls had hand-rubbed panels, there were several fairly nice oils in heavy frames and the carpeting was a rich, dark green, its pile so thick and high that you wondered whether the janitors kept it in shape with a vacuum cleaner or a lawn mower. The total effect was very imposing indeed, especially when you noticed that all the furniture seemed to be genuine antiques.

Boyer was a tall man, dressed in loose brown tweeds cut in the English manner. Even his ox-blood oxfords looked like Saville Row, handmade and bench-turned by an exclusive bootmaker. He had pale amber eyes and a long jaw and sorrel-tinted hair, and the backs of his hands were freckled. His cravat was a work of art. He was standing with his back to the velour-draped windows, facing Shannon. Apparently he had been interrupted at a game of solitaire, the cards still laid out in a serrated pattern on his desk. That was one way to pass the time when you were alone.

Shannon came directly to the point. "I'm looking for a kid named Frank Little."

"Frank Little?"

"A teller at the Third National. You know him."

"Oh, that Frank Little." Boyer smiled. "Why?"

"Because I'm worried about his health."

"Is he sick?"

Shannon took the gun out of his waistband. "Look, Tex, you may have the eyes and ears of the world working for you but right now there's nothing between you and a slug out of this rod except a couple of straight answers."

"Isn't that a little melodramatic, Shannon?"

"Melodramatic as hell, yes. And I mean every word of it. I'm just itching to let somebody have it and it could be you. It will be you if you want it that way."

Boyer massaged his long jaw. He did not seem particularly disturbed. "You wouldn't get very far afterward."

"That's my worry."

"You've got lots of them, haven't you, Shannon?"

"A few," Shannon admitted. "You've probably heard of me, though, so you know I seldom let worries worry me ahead of time. They used to call me Old One-At-A-Time Shannon. To burn you or not to burn you is the immediate problem, and the hell with the future. It can take care of itself after I've taken care of you." He lifted the gun and drew a casual bead on the gambler.

Boyer shrugged. "I don't know where Frank Little is. Does that answer your question?"

"It wouldn't, even if it were the truth."

"I'm not in the habit of lying when there's a gun aimed at me," Boyer said. "It would be foolhardy. You know that."

"All I know is, you put the squeeze on the Little punk in order to get hold of one of Duquesne's checks. I know where the check was found. Therefore it's very logical that you had something to do with my skipper's death. You see why I wouldn't mind shooting you?"

"Quite. What I don't see is what good it would do you."

"Captain Grady was my best friend."

"And presuming I was implicated in his murder, you'd throw away your own life to avenge him?"

"You're talking too much without saying anything," Shannon had ice in his voice. "Where is Frank Little?"

"I'm a professional gambler," Boyer said. "Figuring all the odds, I can't see you doing any shooting with a roomful of people on the other side of that door."

"You're wrong, Boyer."

"If I am, then go ahead and shoot."

Shannon squeezed his trigger. The automatic bucked in his fist and gunsound rocketed around the room, bounced off the walls like rolling thunder. Boyer got an astonished look on his face, staggered a little, grunted and fell over on his back. Boyer wasn't any more astounded than Shannon, because Shannon hadn't shot within inches of the guy. He ran across the office, kneeled alongside the fallen man and saw blood leaking out of his chest.

Boyer's pale amber eyes opened, looked up at Shannon. "So you really did it!"

"Like hell I did!" Shannon yelled. "You got it in the back—through the windows. Now will you talk, God damn it?"

Boyer opened his mouth to say something, and blood filled it. A bubble formed on his lips and burst. Then his pale eyes were staring at Shannon without comprehension, without seeing anything. He was dead.

The door banged in behind Shannon. He came upright and whirled, lifting his gun. The headwaiter was standing there at the threshold with his mouth open, his jaw slack and a nickel plated revolver held in both hands. Both hands were not enough to keep the weapon steady. He was shaking so that the muzzle of the gun described an arc as wide as an oscillating fan. "Get-get 'em up!"

Shannon started walking toward the guy.

The doorway was suddenly filled with an acre of blue uniform, and a hand as big as a quarter of beef sprouted out and knocked the headwaiter's gun spinning.

"So now what the hell goes on here?" this new arrival demanded. He was a big harness bull. Shannon thought he had never seen one so large in all directions. He kept his eyes on Shannon all the while he was trying to unbutton the flap of his belt holster. The headwaiter was squealing like a pig under a fence. He kept pointing to Boyer's body on the green carpet. The harness bull uttered an oath from deep in his chest and finally got his holster flap unfastened.

Shannon took two more slow steps forward. "Look, copper, I'm dropping my gun, see?" He let it fall to the floor. "I didn't shoot the guy. He was gunned from behind, through the window over there."

"Says you."

"All right, am I trying to run away?" Shannon deliberately turned his back, went over and sat at the big desk in the middle of the room. His elbow disturbed the little piles of cards in Boyer's solitaire game as he picked up the phone, but he didn't think Boyer would mind.

The cop had finally got his service .38 out. "Unh-unh, mister. Leave it lay."

"The hell with you," Shannon said. "I'm calling Headquarters." Outside, in the tea room, women were screaming and the lower tones of men's voices played a sort of baritone obligato, but miraculously nobody came to the open door. The harness bull's partner was probably fending them off, herding them out, Shannon thought. He got Headquarters. "Shannon talking, Yes, ex-Lieutenant John J. Shannon. A killing at the Ticker Club. I'm here and so are a couple of flatties." He cradled the phone.

The bull by the door cuffed the bleating headwaiter outside, closed the door and stared at Shannon. "Say, what is this?"

"This," Shannon told him, "is what Sherman said war was." He put his good hand flat on the desk, further disturbing the scattered cards, and leaned forward. "You look like a smart copper to me. Are you?"

The big bull's eyes twinkled. "Is there such a thing?"

Shannon chuckled. "Those are my sentiments exactly! I've always said the same thing." He sobered. "Now look, pal, this thing could be turned into the God damnedest frame you ever saw. I want a witness before the big brass gets here and messes things up."

"I'm listening."

"I took a shot at Boyer, there, but I was bluffing. I deliberately missed him, get it?"

"It don't look to me like you missed him."

"I did, though. I shot through those drapes at the open window. I was trying to scare the bastard. Somebody must have been standing outside with a gun almost at Boyer's back, listening. They shot at the same time I did. Boyer went down."

The cop keeping one eye on Shannon, sidled over to the windows. "The way you tell it, there should ought to be two holes in these here drapes then, hunh?"

"Right."

"Well, there ain't."

"Now, look—"

"There ain't no holes at all."

"The hell you say!" Shannon got up and went over to the windows. The cop was right. There wasn't a sign of a hole. It seemed impossible that both slugs could have found a parting in the drapes, yet apparently they had.

"See?" the harness bull said.

Shannon's stomach crawled. For a minute he thought he was going to be sick. There wasn't a thing between him and a sure-fire murder rap but the possibility that the lethal slug would not match his gun. By this time he wasn't even sure that he hadn't killed Boyer himself. He looked at the cop. "But he was shot in the back, I tell you!"

"Sure. You shot him there."

A sudden commotion at the door drew the cop's eyes for a split second. Shannon made a fist of his good hand and hit him square on the button. It was like hitting the side of a box car, but the bull was sufficiently jolted to drop his gun. Shannon went through the drapes without knowing whether or not there was anything more than thin air on the other side.

There was, though. It was a fire escape landing. Frances McGowan's head and shoulders were sticking out of an adjoining window. She waved urgently. "This way, Shan." Then she withdrew, turtle fashion.

Shannon ducked in after her. It was the ladies' rest room, although fortunately no ladies were resting in it at the time. Shannon and Fran went out of it, Shannon blushing furiously, Frances as perfectly composed as if she always took company with her when she had to go.

No matter how hard he tried, Shannon could never quite remember afterward how they managed to reach the street and Fran's waiting cab without being stopped.

"What happened in there?" Frances demanded.

Shannon looked gloomily out the cab window. They were heading out Seventh. "A guy got shot."

"No!"

"Well, he did." The corners of his mouth drooped and his dark eyes were feverish. "I missed him, I tell you—I missed him a mile. My slug didn't come anywhere near him."

"That means you did shoot at him, though," Fran said. "Maybe you'd better start at the beginning. Some of this doesn't seem to make much sense."

He told her about Boyer, and the harness bull, and all the rest of it. "There was a hole in his chest big enough to drive a truck through, where the slug came—" His own words hit him like a fist. He yelled at the hacker. "Hey, wait! I want a phone!"

The cab pulled into a loading zone and Shannon got out, raced across the sidewalk and slammed into a booth in a corner drugstore. Cursing gustily, he got the *Telegram,* the city desk, and finally Jack Runyon. "Jack, this is Shannon."

"My-oh-my!" Runyon marveled.

Shannon took a breath. "Listen, pal, I don't know how good a friend you are of mine but I'm handing you one hell of a beat if you can get there to cover it in time. Tex Boyer just got himself shot. Dead."

"I heard about it. I was just going over."

"Well, look. Somewhere in that room there should be a bullet. It went clear through him but I was too stupid to think about that at the time."

"You? Stupid? Explain that, please."

Shannon reviled him without rancor. "Get hold of the harness bull that I bopped and he'll tell you what I said. I even left my gun there. But if that slug gets kicked around and lost, well, I don't stand any more chance than snowflakes in hell. This is my neck, chum. I'm putting it in your hands."

"It feels like a very rough neck," Runyon said. Then, crisply: "I'll look into it," he promised. "Thanks for the tip, Shannon—and thanks for trusting me." He rang off.

Shannon called Headquarters and caught Gus Vogel. He told Gus the same story. Vogel was pessimistic. "You been kind of screwy here lately, John J. Maybe your eye ain't so good as it used to be. Your shooting eye, that is. What I mean is, maybe you drilled the guy yourself without knowing it."

"He was facing me, I tell you!" Shannon shouted. "For Christ's sake don't you suppose I know the difference between a guy's face and his back? So if he was looking straight at me, how the hell could I shoot him through the spine so the slug would come out the front of his chest?"

Vogel made blubbery sounds, playing a tune on his lower lip with a blunt forefinger. This caused a very peculiar noise to come over the wire. Presently he said, "Sometimes slugs do some awful funny things, John J."

"Like going around in circles?"

"Well, now, I wouldn't go so far as to say that, maybe. But still and all, you ain't got no witnesses to prove you and him was facing each other."

"That's what I'm trying to tell you!" Shannon groaned. "You get down there and find that slug, hear me? Also my gun. And watch O'Meara. Watch everybody that even touches the things, because it could be just a matter of dropping a little chunk of lead down the nearest sewer whether they gas me or not."

"Aw," Vogel said, "don't be gruesome, John J."

Shannon had to try three times before he finally managed to prong the receiver. He felt slightly giddy.

Frances, no doubt suspecting that Shannon might be trying to outsmart her again, came in through the drug store's front door and met him as he emerged from the phone booth. "That was a clever trick you pulled last time," she commented. "What was all the rush?"

He told her. "And that reminds me," he added. "How come you happened to be at the Ticker Club? I thought I ditched you at the Third National."

"I thought that was what you'd try to do," she nodded. "So I just went around to the side door myself and kept my eyes open." She batted these eyes, ingenuously. "Smart, hunh?"

"All right, so you're brainy."

She smiled. "Then you got in a cab and I followed you in mine. What was the argument you had with your hacker in that alley?"

"He was just a jerk with ideas," Shannon said. "I picked him up once for beating his wife. He was still sore about it." He gave Frances a dour look. "So you tailed me around like a female private dick hunting divorce evidence and ended up in a ladies' room. Did you think you'd find me there?"

She shook her head. "I couldn't stand outside the office door, listening, could I? No. Too conspicuous. That sort of thing could create comment even in a tea room. So I remembered there was a fire escape outside the ladies' you should pardon the expression, 'john'." She cast down her eyes, demurely. "And I thought maybe I could help you in case you got in a jam. It worked out pretty well, didn't it?"

He snapped his fingers. "The guy that shot Boyer was out there on that fire escape. You see anybody?"

"Nope. He could have dropped to the alley, of course."

"Maybe my slug is in the alley too."

"Goody! Let's go back and find it."

Shannon lifted a hand to smack her, dropped it with a gesture of resignation. "I don't know what the hell I see in you. Maybe Gus is right. Maybe I'm punchy."

"Oh, I don't know," Fran preened herself. "I'm not so bad. I have nice legs."

"Remind me to look at them some time."

"And I don't wear falsies."

"Remind me to look—God damn it," he growled, blushing. He went into the phone booth again and called Ward Duffield at the Hotel Corinthian.

Duffield's voice was as impassive as ever. "I thought you were going to call me this morning, Shannon."

"I had a little trouble. It delayed me."

"Have you seen Floyd?"

Shannon's tone sharpened. "No. Haven't you?"

"I talked to him last night over the phone. He said that he'd found some kind of a lead."

"Did he say what it was?"

"He wouldn't tell me. He wouldn't listen to my advice."

"The damned fool! What's he got you down here for if not to help him? How does he expect anybody to do anything for him if he won't tell us what he's up to?" Shannon glowered at the telephone. Then, "Look, here's something for you. I traced the check to a Third National teller named Frank Little, and from him to Tex Boyer, who fronts the Ticker Club for Nick Lombardi—"

Duffield broke in. "And what does that prove—?"

"Will you let me finish?" Shannon raged. "While I was talking to this Boyer somebody let him have it in the back from the fire escape outside his office window. Gunned him down. He died before he could answer any questions. Would Duquesne do that to me?"

"What do you mean, to you?" Duffield said. "I thought you just told me it was Boyer who was shot."

"It was. But the guy who did it must have been listening, maybe even watching through a slit in the window drapes. His shot came at exactly the right time to blend with mine, so that the two sounded like one—"

"You mean you fired, too?" Duffield cut in.

"Christ, I'm trying to tell you!" Shannon yelled. He explained what had happened, adding: "So it looks as though the job was meant to frame me. I'm asking you if you think Floyd would pull a stunt like that, put me in the middle."

"Has he any reason to?"

"Not that I know of."

Duffield didn't say anything for a moment. Then, "Not because Floyd is my brother, Shannon, but there is a third possibility you seem to have overlooked. Boyer might have been killed because it was feared he would open up to you."

Shannon's brows drew together in thought. "That's an angle," he admitted finally. "The truth is, of course, Boyer had no reason to crack to me except that I was threatening to put the heat on him, but his other party might not have known that."

"That's what I was thinking," Duffield said.

"Well, the hell with it for the time being. What have you been doing?"

The lawyer said, "I've talked to Mayor Argyle."

"What did Argyle have to say?"

"Not a thing. He talks in circles. He's afraid of something, though. That trick parade this morning was more to bolster up his courage than anything else."

"What the hell has he got to be afraid of? Besides losing the election, that is."

Duffield's voice rasped in something that might have been a chuckle. "If we can find that out I think we'll have something to get our teeth into."

"Well," Shannon said, "I'll try to keep in touch with you. Watch the newspapers. If I get picked up on this last kill I'm going to need a damned good mouthpiece." He hung up and went out.

Frances was waiting patiently. "Now," she asked sweetly, "will you treat me to an ice cream soda?"

Shannon said, "Nuts! I need a drink."

She looked at him speculatively out of the corners of her eyes. "I've got a bottle of old bonded Mount Vernon. Never been opened."

"Where, in your purse?"

"At home. I could fix us up some lunch, too." Suddenly she became very serious. "You're tired, Shan. It's time you were getting off the merry-go-round, if only for a little while."

He passed a hand over his eyes. "All right, hon. I've got to think and your place is as good as any." He realized that this had been an ungrateful sound. "Good old Shannon. Always the complete heel." He shifted his broken arm in its sling. "Well, let's go."

They went out and got into the taxi and rode out to Fran's apartment. It was a little after one o'clock. The apartment was a three-story walk-up, not too exclusive, but nice. Frances lived on the second floor. She got her key out of her bag, opened the door, took three steps inside before she noticed the guy sitting in her best chair. Shannon, right behind her, felt something hard shoved against his right kidney.

CHAPTER SIX

SHANNON, WITH THAT LETHALLY threatening pressure against his kidney, stood perfectly still. He looked at the first man, the one in the chair. This was none other than Sticky, the tall lean gun who worked for Big Nick Lombardi and aspired to become an airplane pilot. Sticky was nursing a rod in his lap. He seemed bored.

The guy behind Shannon gave him a quick frisk. "Okay, Sticky, he's clean."

The irrepressible Frances said, "Well, isn't this lovely? I adore informal parties, don't you?" She started to run toward the bedroom and the guy behind Shannon put a heel on the throw rug, jerked it. Frances fell flat on her face.

Shannon looked down at her somberly. "You should have known better, kitten."

She rolled over. In falling, her skirt had rucked up several inches above the tops of her sheer stockings. She had been right in her contention that she had nice legs. They were very nice legs indeed. Sticky seemed fascinated by them. Frances scrambled up on her knees. "Well, I like that! I should have known better, should I?" She glared indignantly at Shannon. "Haven't you any manners?"

"No, I've got boils. Sticky, and this guy behind me."

The guy behind him took his gun away from Shannon's kidney and clipped him across the back of the neck with it. Shannon went down on all fours, cursing groggily.

"Nick wants to see you, Irish," Sticky said.

"What about?'

"By me. He just said to bring you."

"Well, I won't go, see?" Shannon lurched to his feet, helped Frances upright. "If you bastards are going to do any shooting you can do it here."

Sticky said softly, "The little lady too?" He blinked his eyes lazily, letting them wander over Fran's body. She reddened under his frank scrutiny, as though he had X-ray vision. He said, "She looks like a nice number, Shannon. If she belonged to me I don't believe I'd want her hurt."

Shannon's voice was thick. "You'll leave her alone if I go with you?"

"For a while."

"All right, you've made a deal."

Frances suddenly quit pretending that she wasn't scared. "No, Shan, they'll trick you!"

"I haven't got anything to lose," Shannon said. "If they wanted to they could burn us both down right here. I'll take a chance. And don't you go calling copper, either, understand?"

"No," Sticky purred, "no coppers, babe." He and Shannon and the little guy with the ugly face went out the door. Sticky had a sedan across the street. The little guy drove this. Sticky sat with Shannon in the tonneau, all the way out Wilshire to the modernistic glass-and-redwood apartment building where Lombardi lived. Lombardi was getting his hair trimmed in a damask-paneled living room when Shannon and his captors arrived. Big Nick was on a chaise longue, propped up among a flock of cushions, reading the morning papers and smoking a heavy black cigar. The whole room smelled of lilac vegetal.

Sticky and Sour-Puss pushed Shannon in ahead of them, so that Lombardi could look at him without turning his head. They then backed away, like courtiers before a throne. The barber held a double mirror for the big guy to look in. Lombardi peered at himself with affection and said, "Okay, Sam. Very nice."

"That's a matter of opinion," Shannon remarked audibly.

Nobody answered him. Sam dusted the fat man's neck with talc, removed the hair cloth, his tools and himself. Lombardi folded his porcine bulk more tightly in his brocaded red satin robe and then, settling himself, regarded Shannon with eyes like liquid velvet. "You're beginning to annoy me, Shannon."

Shannon exhibited his trick of unpocketing and lighting a cigarette with his one good hand. He deliberately dropped the match on four thousand dollars' worth of carpet. "That's tough," he exhaled smoke, derisively.

Sour-puss came over and picked up the match and placed it in an ash tray. "Just like your broad said," he grunted. "You got no manners."

Lombardi continued. "It isn't only Tex Boyer, it's the Ticker Club." His soft voice held regret, but not for Boyer. "That was a sweet spot, Shannon. Very profitable."

"Well, what's the matter with it?"

"Boyer's killing was sort of unexpected. The cops got there before the boys had time to rearrange the furniture, so to speak. If you know what I mean. Offhand, I'd say the damage amounted to somewhere in the neighborhood of a hundred grand."

"Classy neighborhood, that."

"Have you got a hundred grand, Shannon?"

"Sure. Will you take my personal check or do you want it all in dollar bills?"

"I'm not playing any more, Shannon."

"Then lay off asking me whacky questions like have I got a hundred G's. You know goddamned well I haven't. How come the drop got raided? I thought you were wired to the cops?"

"These weren't the right cops." Lombardi sucked on his cigar, blew a smoke ring as thick and greasy as his face. "So you killed Boyer. Why?"

"I didn't kill him. Maybe I would have, but I didn't."

Big Nick patted his shiny black curls. "Can you prove this? I believe the slug wasn't found."

Shannon took a deep breath. "Meaning one of your mob picked it up first?"

"Don't be silly. But let us say that one of them did. He would be a very valuable witness for you, no?"

Shannon looked around the room, not really seeing it, feeling only the constriction of the four walls, like a newly caged jaguar. A little desperately he said. "All right, I know when I'm licked. What have I got that you want?"

A knock on the door interrupted Lombardi's answer. Sour-Puss went over and opened it, and a woman came in. She was a beautiful woman if you liked them statuesque and full-blown and red-haired. Especially if you didn't mind the obvious fact that the red hair was a henna job, very expensive, very adroit, and only a trifle dark at the roots. Her face was that of a slightly corrupt Madonna, the complexion creamy without too much make-up, the mouth artfully painted, the amethyst eyes a little too experienced. Somebody had paid a lot of money for her clothes and she wore them well. Shannon knew her by sight. Her name was Karen Kane, she was a graduate of Vassar, she had been a stripper in burlesque and she was currently being kept by Big Nick Lombardi, not entirely as an ornament.

She crossed over to the fat guy, the muscles of her sleek legs and flanks rippling under the clinging dress, her hips graceful in the way a stripper learns by rote. "Nick, darling, I thought I might go down and buy that mink coat this afternoon. It's seven thousand, not six. Alterations, you know. Have you an extra thousand with you?"

"Six I already gave you," Lombardi said. "That was the price you told me. What's with this extra grand you want?"

"I just explained it. Alterations, darling."

He stood up. "Two things I won't stand for, baby. One is you interrupting me when I'm busy. You've been warned about that before."

"Oh, I'm sorry, Nick."

"The other is you taking me for a sucker," Lombardi's voice was like silk being torn. "I checked on that coat. It's six G's *with* alterations. I gave you the dough to buy it. So now you're short a grand. You want to know why? I'll tell you. You dropped a thousand bucks at roulette a couple of nights ago. I wouldn't care, only you didn't drop it at one of my places, you lost it at a Duquesne layout."

"So you've been having your goons follow me."

He hit her across the face with his open hand hard enough to stagger her a little. His fat fingers left imprints on her cheek. Her breasts rose and fell swiftly with her breathing. Nick said, "Get out, sweetheart. We'll talk about this some other time."

"When you've got your collection of buggy whips handy, I presume?"

He hit her with his other hand. "Get out."

"Yes, darling," she said meekly. "Sorry I bothered you. You will forgive me, won't you?" She went out.

Lombardi sat down again, as unemotionally as if nothing had happened. He regarded Shannon. "You asked me what you've got that I want." He smiled. "I like running this town, Shannon. I want to keep on running it. Things were going along nicely until you started messing around; the election was all being straightened out, everything. Why couldn't you keep your nose clean?"

"My skipper was killed. Not only that, he was made to look like a rat."

"You can't hurt a dead man, Shannon."

"The hell you can't."

Lombardi took a new line. "Where can I find Floyd Duquesne?"

"I don't know. Maybe I could find out."

Sticky spoke up for the first time. "He's handing you a stall Nick. Why not just let me handle him?"

"Don't be impatient, Sticky," Lombardi said mildly. "We're doing all right." He turned his liquid velvet eyes to Shannon's face. "There's a murder rap against you. There's the little matter of a hundred grand I figure you've cost me. Tex Boyer can be replaced, the same as your dead skipper can be replaced, but the other things are not so easily arranged."

Shannon said, "So what do I have to do?"

"Just two things, my friend. Two simple little things. Locate Duquesne for me," he raised a chubby finger, ticked it off. Then he raised the mate to it. "And bring me the stuff your skipper was killed for."

"And if I don't?"

"Then it will be just too bad for a certain little lady."

Shannon's throat tightened. "You mean you've got Fran McGowan?'

"What do you think?"

Shannon whirled on the lazy-eyed Sticky. "You dirty stinking double-crossing son of a bitch. You said you'd leave her alone if I came along quietly!"

"Well, haven't I? Haven't I been with you every minute, pal?" Sticky scratched his chin with his gun muzzle.

"But if I don't know where either Duquesne or the stuff is? What then?" Shannon asked, a little wildly.

Lombardi smiled. "Then I'm sure you'll work very hard finding it out, Mister Shannon. Won't you, Mister Shannon?" He gestured. "You may go, now."

Shannon stumbled out of the room. There may have been people on the stairs, if so he didn't see them. Maybe the lobby of the apartment building was crawling with hoods and hangers-on; Shannon was not aware of them. He didn't see anything until afternoon sunlight blinded him and he knew that he was on the street, walking aimlessly. He went into the first bar he came to, sat down in a booth and put his head down on his good arm. The waiter had to speak to him three times before he realized the guy was asking him what he would have to drink.

"Rye," he said. "Mount Vernon." That made him think of Frances McGowan, and the unopened bottle she had mentioned having in her apartment. He shook as though with a chill.

Many drinks later, the shaking had gone and the pounding throb in his temples went away. Other guys with that much liquor in them would have been blotto, or at least pleasantly plastered. Shannon was cold sober. He was so sober that he thought the waiter must have come to the wrong booth when the guy approached him, leaned down, winked, leered and said, "There's a lady upstairs, a redhead, in one of the private dining rooms wants to see you, pal."

"I don't know any redheads. What the hell is this, a creep joint? You think I'm a mark? Bring on my check and go do your pimping somewhere else."

The guy's face darkened. "I've busted drunks with bung-starters for calling me less than that. You I'll pass up on account you got a bum flipper," he looked at Shannon's broken arm in its sling. "I don't pick on cripples. Besides, the dame give me ten bucks tip to bring you the message. Your name's Shannon, ain't it?"

"Yes."

"Then you're the one, all right. She said tell you Karen wants to see you. She said you'd know who she was."

Shannon stood up. "Karen?" Then he got it. He threw a ten dollar bill on the table. "That cover my drinks?"

"With some change left over, pal."

"Keep it. Show me the stairs to this private room."

The waiter pointed to a door. "Room A, second floor."

Shannon went up to room A and walked in, warily. Big Nick Lombardi's Karen Kane came forward, put her arms around him, pressed herself very tightly against him and kissed him on the mouth, her parted lips moist and warm and demanding.

The room was small, cozy, intimate and very dimly lighted. It had a table in a sort of alcove, with one chair opposite a leather-upholstered bench. The bench was as long and about as wide as a couch; with a mattress it could double for a Pullman lower. There was a fifth of Scotch on the table. Vat 69, but although it had been opened it did not seem to have been depleted by so much as one drink. And there was no odor of liquor to be detected on Karen Kane's sultry breath. What she was doing was not because her inhibitions had been melted by alcohol. Maybe she had never had any inhibitions in the first place, Shannon thought. But she had everything else a woman needs, including technique.

After a while she withdrew her mouth from Shannon's. Her eyes were heavy-lidded. "Like it?"

"I'd like it better if I knew the reason."

"Why does there have to be a reason? When a woman decides she wants a man to make love to her, that's reason enough." She kissed him again.

He couldn't deny that it stirred him. The redhead had qualities that would have stirred any man under the age of ninety. "I still don't get the pitch, though," he said, a little gustily.

"Why bother?" she smiled. "Have a drink."

"I don't go for Scotch."

"Maybe you don't go for red hair, either?" Her eyes measured him. "I could always dye it another color." She sat on the upholstered, sofa-like bench and pulled him down alongside her and drew his good arm around her waist. "You know, Shannon, you're rather a handsome guy in a dissolute sort of way."

"And you're Nick Lombardi's private property."

She said, "That fat swine!" and once more put her mouth on Shannon's. Her cheeks were a little flushed, now.

Shannon cooperated briefly and instinctively. Then reason took hold and he pushed her away. "Whoever said dames were devious was crazy as hell. They're as direct as a straight line."

"Alluding to me as a clinical specimen?" she drawled.

He nodded, poured himself a stiff jolt of the Vat 69 and gulped it, grimaced at the smoky peat-bog flavor.

She ran her hands over her seductive curves. "Find a straight line on me anywhere. You can't." Her expression was challenging, her voice a throaty dare.

Shannon considered the invitation, was tempted, and resisted it. "I wasn't talking about your body, baby. I wasn't even thinking about it."

"Most men do when they see it." She settled back, studying him. "You don't look like a Puritan."

"God forbid."

"Kiss me, then."

He eluded this by having another drink. He wanted time to weigh the situation and to take a greater advantage of it than what she was offering. "There's no hurry, is there?"

"This is sort of a new experience for me," she remarked. "A man playing hard to get. Maybe that's the trouble. Maybe you prefer to be the pursuer instead of the pursued. Maybe I'm too forthright for you."

"Not at all. I like frankness."

She began to look a little irritated. "Don't get the idea that I'm promiscuous just because I asked you up here. I may be a bitch but I'm an exclusive bitch. I'm no pushover except when I want to be." She narrowed her eyes at him. "Are you going to kiss me or aren't you?"

"Your kind of kisses don't stop with just kissing," he grinned. "Not with me they wouldn't."

"I might not struggle very hard, Shannon."

"I'm sure you wouldn't. But would you tell Nick Lombardi about it after it happened?"

"No, if that's what's holding you back. You needn't be afraid Nick would find out about it."

Shannon patted her knee. "I'm not scared of Lombardi. But if you don't intend to tell him that you and I had a little party, I can't see what good this would do you."

"What do you mean by that?"

He laughed. "Look, Tutz, I'll tell you how I analyze you. Lombardi slapped your face, twice, in front of witnesses. He humiliated you. You're not the type to take it without getting even, are you? Whatever else you may be, you're proud. And like I said a minute ago, you're direct, too. After Nick slapped you and you walked out of the room, I think you listened at the door. I think you eavesdropped on what he said to me. You found out that he and I are enemies. I think you tailed me when I left his apartment. You saw me come in this joint, so you came in, too, by a side door. You fixed up the private room setup and sent me a message you wanted to see me. Throwing yourself at me is your way of getting even with Big Nick for slapping you around. You're supposed to be his exclusive property, so what's a better way of hurting him than to two-time him with a guy he hates?"

"Quite a speech, Shannon. Practically a lecture."

"So I'm gabby. Excuse it please. The point is, what the hell kind of revenge would it be on Nick if he doesnt know it happened?"

"*I'd* know it," she said. Her smile was feline. "So would you. We'd both have the laugh on the fat louse. Kiss me, Shannon."

He kissed her, rather perfunctorily. "You're a swell dish, Karen, but it takes two to make a party and I'm damned poor company just now. I've got a busted arm, my best friend has been murdered, I'm kind of under the gun for killing Tex Boyer, and Lombardi has kidnapped my girl. It's pretty hard to forget things like that."

"I suppose it is," she admitted. "The spot you're in is just a little incompatible with romance." She stood up. "All right, Shannon, I understand. No hard feelings."

"Not that you aren't attractive," he said. "You are."

She accepted this not as a compliment but as an established fact. "I know I am. Well, some other time, maybe. I think I could go for you, my friend."

"I like you too, dumpling." He was choosing his words very carefully, for effect, although he made them sound sincere. "And I don't blame you for wanting to get even with Lombardi for what he did to you. Maybe you will get even with him. Maybe you'll find a better way than the one you had in mind."

She made a thoughtful mouth. "Perhaps an idea along that line has already occurred to me."

His heart started to pound. He hoped it wasn't loud enough for her to hear it. He said casually. "Yes?" and wondered if this was going to be the break he'd been fishing for.

"Lombardi had your girl kidnapped," she said. "Why not turn the tables on him, fight fire with fire? Do to him what he's done to you, Shannon."

"Are you suggesting I ought to kidnap you?"

Her laughter held very little mirth. "You could burn me at the stake and he wouldn't shed a tear. No, I meant his daughter."

"Daughter?" Shannon's eyes popped open.

"You didn't know he had one, did you? Not many people do know. It's a fact, though. Maria is her name, a beautiful kid; a little too beautiful for her own good. Demure to look at, but very, very modern."

"What do you mean, modern?"

"An euphemism, Shannon. If you want me to be blunt about it. I mean she's got more than a slight nympho tendency. Nick was worrying his heart out over it until he enrolled her at St. Catherine's."

"That girls' boarding school up on Western?"

She nodded. "Very strict supervision, no boys allowed inside the gates. Maria is Nick's weak spot, Shannon, his heel of Achilles. Get her and you'll stab him in the only place where he's vulnerable. He'll eat out of your hand. He'll crawl—and I want to be there to see it."

Shannon's nostrils pinched in. "Christ!" he breathed softly. Then, "Thanks, Karen." He made for the door, stopped, turned and kissed her almost savagely.

This time she was the one who broke away. "On your horse, Shannon, I don't need that, now. I'm square with Lombardi and I'm going to enjoy it a lot more than the other idea I had." She smiled a little crookedly. "Good luck, Irish. I hope you get your Frances back. Whatever danger she's in, I almost wish I could trade places with her." She gave Shannon a push.

He left her and went back down to the bar, had the waiter call a cab for him and stood in the cool dimness of the front door until it came. There was no use taking unnecessary chances. He couldn't go on being immune forever. The broken arm hanging on him like a dead weight was almost a sure means of identification. It might as well have been a flag.

The cab pulled up and the hacker turned out to be Osterwicz. "Well, hel-lo, there!" he said. "Funny thing, I was just thinking about you."

"You must have a radio in your car."

"That's right, pal. Boy, what they're saying about a guy name of Shannon."

"How much are they offering for me?"

"Not a cent, the heels."

"Then I guess I can trust you for a while, hunh?"

Osterwicz held up two fingers. "You and me are just like that, pal."

"Why? Because I kicked you in the stomach?"

"Well, yes and no. It proved something I been worrying about for a long time. Now I don't have to worry no more, see? Besides, I kind of admire you. We got something in common. You're a nonconformist and so am I. I seen that word in a book once. It means a guy which does things his own way and to hell with what everybody else thinks."

"You may have something there," Shannon said. He looked both ways along the street to see if anybody had watched him pile into the cab. No one was paying him the slightest attention. He said, "There's a pawnbroker over on East Fifth named Rasnikoff. Know the place?"

Osterwicz said he did. After a while the hacker pulled up in front of Rasnikoff's place. It was the usual east-of-Main hock shop; an interior so dark you could scarcely see your hand in front of your eyes, grimy showcases and windows piled high with a heterogeneous miscellany comprising everything from an automobile jack to a silk topper. Shannon ducked inside, fast.

Old Rasnikoff appeared, gnome-like, from behind a stack of boxes on a counter. He had a white beard, like Santa Claus, and he shaved his head like a Prussian army officer.

Actually he was an emigre Czarist Russian, and his rumbling voice reminded you of thunder in a rain barrel.

"Well, well!" he pushed steel-rimmed glasses high on his forehead. "Is being my old friend Shannon. A long time you have staying away, isn't it?"

"Hello, Boris," Shannon said. "I want a gun."

The guy recoiled. "Now waiting just one moments. You should knowing I can't let you have it no guns. Is being against the law, unless you shall showing me a permit?"

"Permit be damned. I want a gun."

"These coppers, all the time they watching me, they come and taking numbers from the guns I have buying. They telling me I shall sell a gun without the customers will producing a permit, I have being tossed in the can." He sighed, eyeing Shannon obliquely. "You wanting that I should being in jail, Shannon?"

Shannon leaned forward. "I hate to remind people of the favors I've done them, but there was a kid once who might have turned into an alley rat and a hophead if I hadn't got him out of his first jam. Something about a stolen hot-rod, as I recall. He straightened out after that and went to college and later he enlisted, won a Distinguished Flying Cross in the South Pacific. He's buried in a hero's grave on Okinawa."

"I have a very fine Luger," the Russian said. "Is being funny coincidence, the police do not having its numbers. Nine millimeter, sixty dollars."

"A dozen?" Shannon said. "Anyway it's too heavy."

"There is also being possible a very fine Colt .32."

"The cops missed that one, too, I'll bet."

"You should expecting them to being perfect and not making no mistakes ever?"

Shannon leered. "Okay, Boris. So I was a cop until last night and I made plenty of mistakes." He inspected the Colt, found it all right, picked up two extra clips and put a twenty dollar bill on the counter.

Shannon walked out of the grimy store, his eyes half ashamed of what he was about to attempt, but his mouth was set in a thin hard line. He got in the cab.

Osterwicz gave him a worried look. "Where to now, pal?"

"You know where St. Catherine's is? It's a boarding school for girls."

"Now look," Osterwicz said, "it ain't none of my business, I know, but it don't seem to me like this is hardly the time for romance. Or am I wrong?"

"Romance?" Shannon sucked in his breath. "For what I'm about to do they put people in the lethal chamber." He leaned back and closed his eyes. "All right, get going."

Osterwicz wheeled the cab in a wide U-turn and headed west through thickening traffic. After a while there wasn't any more traffic because the street they were on was a private drive, deadended by St. Catherine's itself.

Shannon got out at the century-old wrought iron gates. He was trembling again. He wished he had another drink, even of Scotch. There was a tight knot in his stomach, and for a minute he fought down a reflex to be actively sick. It passed. He pulled out a depleted roll of bills, laid a twenty on the meter. "All right, boy, you'd better scram now."

"Unh-unh. I'll stick."

Shannon looked at him. "You're a funny guy, fella." He was suddenly embarrassed. "Look, I don't know why you feel the way you do, but I want you to know I appreciate it."

"Leave us not slop over and get gushy, pal."

"You son of a bitch," Shannon said without heat. Then, "This is one time when you can't do me any good by sticking. You'll only get yourself in a jam. So blow, there's a good guy."

"Okay, sucker, it's your neck." The hacker snatched the twenty, stuck it in his pants pocket, clashed his gears and wheeled the cab viciously. Shannon watched the taxi vanish around the nearest corner. Then he walked through the wrought iron gates. He felt curiously lonely.

It was a big gray stone building, vine-clad, with recessed stained-glass windows and heavy oaken doors. It had all the dignity of a cathedral and was great deal more exclusive. The broad expanse of lawn was dotted here and there with carefully tended flower beds whose colors were subdued in keeping with the surroundings.

Shannon mounted to the wide stone veranda and tugged at the bell pull. A deeply religious man underneath, he felt as though he were about to ravish a convent. His hat was in his hand when the door opened.

The woman who smiled out at him was old, too, though not in the same way as the gardener. She could have been a dowager queen; she could have been St. Catherine herself. She looked at Shannon and he felt as though she were seeing the very soul of him. He hoped that the woman wouldn't smell the whiskey on his breath.

"I'd like to speak to Maria Lombardi," he said carefully, trying to keep his eyes from looking shifty. "It's about her father."

"Maria is in class at present."

"I'm sorry. This is rather important."

"Come in, please." Her voice was deep, filled with an inner calm that Shannon envied because he knew that in his own lifetime he would never attain anything like it.

He followed her into a pleasantly dim study. The walls were lined with books, and, like the paneling, the books looked as if they had been there forever. The only modern notes in the room were a telephone and an intercommunicating box with a number of keys and a speaker that also did duty as a transmitter. The woman depressed a key, spoke into the box. It answered scratchily that Maria Lombardi was, at the moment, taking phys-ed in the gymnasium. The woman closed the key, smiled again at Shannon and went away. Her footfalls made no sound whatever.

Shannon looked at the intercom box, touched it, tested it to make sure it was cut off; he wanted no electronic eavesdropping on what he was going to do. He lifted the phone from its cradle to find out if it went through a PBX switchboard somewhere in the school building. It's dial tone told him that it did not. It was a direct outside line. This brought a glint of satisfaction into his eyes. He examined the windows, even tiptoed over and inspected the only door. Everything suited him.

Then he took his gun out, and, holding it between his knees, jacked a cartridge into the firing chamber. This done, he placed the gun on the desk, under his hat. He wanted a cigarette but decided that smoking would be out of place here. He decided that he was a hell of an odd guy to be unwilling to desecrate the room with tobacco smoke when he had already defiled it by bringing in a gun. His fingers drummed the desk nervously.

Presently the door opened and a girl came in, closing it after her. She was in shorts and a halter, and while she may have been only seventeen-going-on-eighteen she was as physically mature as she would ever need to be. More so, maybe. Dark curls, reminiscent of Big Nick Lombardi's own, though infinitely more beautiful, made damp little ringlets on her brow and about her ears. Dark eyes, wide-spaced and intelligent, evaluated Shannon. She did not in the least resemble a juvenile delinquent, but then juvenile delinquents seldom do. Shannon thought he had never seen a young girl so completely nubile, so flagrantly feminine. The sheer animal magnificence of her body appalled Shannon just a little. He felt like a guy confronted by an instrument of destruction, a weapon in the possession of a child who did not realize its potentialities for harm either to others or to herself.

"Hello," she said. Her throaty voice was anything but childlike. "You wanted to see me?"

"Yes," he said. "Sit down, please."

She remained standing. The headmistress said it was something about my father."

"Yes. Please sit down. Over here by the desk."

She ignored this. "Has anything happened to him, I hope?"

Shannon gave her a shocked look. He had revised his plans slightly after coming here, because the telephone and the general layout of the room had made it unnecessary to take the girl with him as he'd originally intended. All the plans in the world, though, could not have prepared him for the kind of girl Maria Lombardi was, nor for the remark she had just made.

He wondered if she knew what sort of a guy she had for a father. He wondered if she had inherited Lombardi's cool calculating lack of morals, his utter selfishness. Shannon was afraid that she had. He began to suspect that in Maria there was more of filial hatred than devotion, and the suspicion upset him. For all his outer veneer of toughness, at heart Shannon had a certain respect for the old-fashioned virtues. Cynicism and hardness were all right for adults, but not for a girl as young as this Lombardi kid.

He stared at her. "What do you mean, has anything happened to him—you hope?"

"Oh, skip it." She returned his scrutiny. "I don't think I know you, do I?"

"No, but I'm afraid you're going to." He tried not to think about the gun on the desk and why he had brought it here. He went over to the door and twisted the key in the lock, dropped the key into his pocket, came back to the desk and sat at it.

"Why did you do that?" the girl said.

"Because I don't want us to be interrupted." He made his eyes meet hers, impersonally. "I asked you to sit down in that chair," he indicated it. "Now I'm telling you to."

She obeyed gracefully, smiling. "Mm-m-m-m. Stern, aren't you? A disciplinarian." Her interest shifted. "What's the matter with your arm?"

"I broke it."

"Does it hurt much?" The red tip of her tongue came out, licked at lips even redder.

"It doesn't hurt at all." He sensed that she was disappointed. "Listen, Maria, your father—"

"Are you one of his goons?"

"No, and shut up. Listen carefully to what I—"

"A friend of his?" she persisted.

Shannon scowled. "On the contrary. Does that frighten you?"

"It pleases the hell out of me," she said, not at all flippantly. This made her words sound doubly incongruous, coming so earnestly and so easily from her innocent-looking lips. "Any enemy of my father's is a friend of mine." She trilled laughter at his sudden startled expression. "There's nothing unnatural about a girl despising her father. Happens all the time, particularly if she's got the kind of father I have." She shrugged, imparting deliberately provocative movement to her breasts in the skimpy halter. "You wouldn't happen to have a cigarette, would you?"

"I have this." He lifted his hat off the gun, watched her eyes settle on the black ugliness of it. "I don't want to have to use it, Maria."

You knew she was impressed, but she showed no indication of fear. "Loaded?"

"Yes." Shannon leaned toward her. "Your father has something I want. The only way I can get it back is through you."

She affected a yawn, patted it with a bored hand. Shannon observed, though, that the hand trembled a little. She said, "Maybe I should understand what you're driving at, but I'm afraid I don't. Sorry."

"Maybe you don't have to understand it." He pushed the phone at her. "Just call your father and tell him exactly what you see here."

"And what exactly do I see?"

"A man named Shannon, with a gun, alone with you in a locked room."

She reached for the phone, hesitated. "What would happen if I called the police instead?"

"I'd stop you. I'll be watching you dial."

"And if I screamed?"

"I will have to shoot you," he said. He hoped that she believed that. He was pretty sure that he believed it himself. Barring this one chance now in his hands, there was nothing left to do but punish in retaliation for punishment. An eye for an eye.

She smiled. "You wouldn't shoot me, Mr. Shannon."

"Make that phone call."

"Men don't wantonly destroy beautiful things, except possibly in warfare."

He made a grim mouth. "This is warfare, Maria." He lifted the gun.

"You must hate my father almost as much as I do."

"The phone call, Maria. Make it. Now."

"But you wouldn't kill me. Not even to hurt him."

His eyes grew muddy with mounting anger. "Damn you, I said to call your father. Stop stalling."

"There are other ways to hurt him, Mr. Shannon, better ways—ways that would serve your purpose just as well as shooting me. I want out of here. You could take me with you. You could be the white knight on his charger, saving the fair maiden from durance vile. And winning the maiden's favors for your reward," her voice had sultry significance.

"Quit talking like a little tramp," he said through his teeth. "Pick up that phone."

"So I'm a tramp. So I hate being cloistered in this dump like a nun. That's logical for a tramp, isn't it? And I hate my father for penning me here. Take me out, Mr. Shannon, and when you're tired of me, let me go my own way. Just knowing that he's lost me to the kind of life I want to lead will make my father die a little, inside. That should satisfy you."

"Nothing's going to satisfy me except your making that phone call. I won't tell you again." His face was drawn with tension as he stood up. He played a trump card. "If you make me shoot you, Maria, I promise you my bullet won't kill you. But all the plastic surgery in the world will never make your face beautiful again. Guys will look at you and shudder and turn away."

She lost color, and he knew he had hit a nerve. Fear came into her eyes for the first time. "You—wouldn't."

"You've got one minute to find out."

"Will you make a deal with me, Mr. Shannon? If I call him and say something to him that would shake him even more than what you told me to say, will you—take me out of here when you leave?"

"Make your call. We'll bargain when I see what happens."

She dialed a number, waited, spoke Lombardi's name into the instrument. Presently she said, "Father? Maria. I'm locked up in a room with a man who has a broken arm and a gun; a man who says his name is Shannon." Her face had the vindictive cruelty of a cat's. "He says he's going to force me to go to bed with him. And father, you want to know something? He won't have to force me."

CHAPTER SEVEN

THE GIRL'S VOICE was so sweetly spiteful, so viciously bland with honeyed poison, that Shannon stared at her for a moment with complete incredulity. Then he snatched the telephone out of her hand. "Lombardi?"

Lombardi's answer was a long time coming, as if shock had rendered him temporarily inarticulate. Then, "Shannon, you son of a bitch! God damn you to hell, Shannon!"

"Cursing me will get you nowhere, Lombardi."

The guy's voice shook. "Listen. Listen to me. If you touch Maria I'll cut your heart out, so help me God!"

"That won't give you back your daughter."

"You bastard!" Lombardi raged. "What have you done to her?"

"Nothing—yet."

"Let her go, Shannon. I'm warning you, let her go or I'll kill you."

"That will make two funerals for you to send flowers to. Hers and mine."

Lombardi choked, "You wouldn't Shannon. Christ, you wouldn't do that."

"Wouldn't I?"

"But you'd do other things. She's the kind that would let you."

"So I've noticed."

The guy made horrible strangling sounds in his throat. "Shannon, listen to me. Are you there, Shannon?"

Shannon had anticipated that the fat man would crumble and go to pieces, but there was an anguish in his voice that was unnerving to hear. "Yes, I'm still on the line," Shannon said quickly. "Did you think I was playing, Nick? After what you did to me?"

"What do you want, Shannon? For the love of God, what will buy you off?"

"You know without being told. There's somebody who means just as much to me as Maria means to you. More. I give you my word that unless you do as I say—" The girl had been inching forward, eyes glowing, her tongue darting out to lick at her lips as if tasting unseen blood. On her lovely face was an expression of abysmally cruel pleasure, she was like one in a trance, projecting herself across space to her father's apartment so that she would witness his torture. Shannon put down the phone, slapped her back into her chair. She laughed, stridently.

Lombardi's voice rattled in the phone. "Shannon, what happened? What did you do?"

"Nothing much. She's all right—so far."

"Let me hear her voice."

Shannon put his hand on the gun, looked at the girl. "He wants to hear you say something."

"Of course, darling." She picked up the phone. "I wish you'd stop interrupting me while I'm taking my clothes off, father." No woman had ever spoken more tenderly, or with more malice. Smiling, she gave the phone back to Shannon.

He could hear Lombardi drag air painfully into his lungs, like a drowning man who comes to the surface for the last time before he goes down for keeps. Then, "All right, Shannon, you win."

"I'm glad you see it my way."

"How do we work it, Shannon?" The guy had got hold of himself now, because his voice was a little steadier. "And what about the rest of the setup?"

"The hell with the rest of it. I'll take my chances in an even fight. I don't like the sniping, at all. So here's what you'll do. Listen hard, because I'm only going to say it once."

"I'm listening."

"You'll deliver my girl to Gus Vogel at Headquarters. I don't care how you manage it; that's your problem. Probably she can't drag you into it anyway, but she's smart enough to know better than to blow the whistle on you."

"I understand."

"Good. How long will it take you to get her there?"

"Half an hour. Maybe less. I'll try to make it less."

"I'll give you twenty minutes. Then I'm going to call Gus and find out if you came through. When I hear her voice, and Vogel's, I'll step out."

Shannon contrived a tight little smile for Maria. "Well, that seems to be that. It's not certain yet, but I think everything is going to be all right."

"And when it is?"

She stood up, came toward him. "You're forgetting something."

"Am I? What?"

"A promise, Mr. Shannon. A deal we made."

"Sit down and stop posing. Stop trying to dazzle me with your beautiful little body. I'm no cradle-robber."

"Eighteen is the age of consent," she said.

"Your only seventeen. Sit down."

She sat down and crossed her legs. "About our deal, Mr. Shannon."

"I didn't make any deal with you."

"Yes you did, at least by implication. If everything goes the way you want, you're to take me out of here with you."

"Oh, that," he said. "Now I remember. You want to go your own way, lead a life of your own choosing. You wouldn't like that kind of life, Maria."

"Isn't that for me to say?"

"And there's no money in it these days."

"But there's pleasure."

He grinned. "I've talked with a lot of girls in the racket and they tell me different."

"And there's freedom."

"Not even that, Maria. The syndicates keep pretty tight shackles on their cattle. That's the price of the protection they furnish. And without protection, an independent hustler gets rousted by the cops just about every time she starts walking the streets. You've got the wrong slant on things, kid."

She stared at him, white-lipped. "Meaning you don't intend to take me out of here?"

"That's right."

She lunged for the gun on the desk. He blocked her, sent her crashing back into her chair. She sagged there, her eyes venomous. "I hate you."

"Lots of people do," Shannon admitted. "I'm not a very nice guy. I even try to talk young girls like you out of the notion of becoming prostitutes." He ran squarish fingers through his shock of pepper-and-salt hair. He didn't feel especially hot, but the palm of his hand came away wet with sweat.

"I'm going to get even with you, Shannon."

"It's a risk I guess I'll have to take."

For the next few minutes that seemed endless the girl sat quite still, not speaking, but staring steadily at him. And, meeting her eyes, Shannon realized that her hate had driven every other emotion out of her now.

There was a knock on the door and a cool, detached voice came faintly. "Are you all right, Maria?"

Shannon lifted the gun.

"Quite all right," the girl called back. Her eyes cursed Shannon, and, in a way, he cursed himself, but her reaching for the gun had made him feel a little better. She was her father's own daughter, whether she knew it or not. Shannon thought of Karen Kane and concluded that within a few years Maria would be walking along the same path that Karen had chosen. Big Nick Lombardi didn't seem to have much luck with his women.

Shannon and the girl sat in silence until twenty-five minutes had passed. Then he picked up the phone and dialed Headquarters, asked for Gus Vogel. He could hear Vogel's phone ringing, and the receiver being lifted. He said, "Hello?"

"Hello, Shan." It was unmistakably Fran's voice. "I'm okay."

He breathed a little prayer of relief. "Is Vogel there?"

"Yes."

There was a pause.

Vogel's voice: "What goes on, John J.?"

"Games," Shannon said. "Dirty games. The less you know about them the better. Excuse me a minute, Gus." He put down the phone, delved into his pocket for the key and tossed it at Maria. "I'm through with you. Beat it." The girl went over to the door, unlocked it and ran out, saying something over her shoulder as she vanished. Shannon picked up the telephone again.

Vogel said, "Did I hear somebody say—"

"Yes. Somebody said she would see me in hell for something that just happened. Skip it."

"Well, now, look, John J.," Vogel complained. "I don't like to pry, but—"

"Then don't," Shannon said. "You're still a cop and you've got an old lady to support. What I said to you a moment ago still goes. The less you know about this particular deal, the better."

"That's no way to talk to a friend."

Shannon frowned. "You're wearing a badge that throws friendship out the window. For all you know I may have killed Tex Boyer. I'm on the wanted list and you'd better stay the hell away from me. All I'm asking you to do is to see Frances to some safe spot and tell her to stay there, under cover. No, I don't even want to know the address now. I'll get it later."

Fran's voice: "Are you all right, Shan?"

"Sure, hon. You?"

"Absolutely." She jiggled the hook. "Shan, are you still there? I don't know who the men were, but it's obvious they were working for Lombardi."

"I know that, kitten. Don't let Gus know it, though. He might go blundering around and rock the boat. This is a personal matter. Just go where he tells you and stay put till you hear from me. Will you do that?"

"All right, Shan, but—"

He cut her off, stood up, put the gun in his pocket. It didn't occur to him that he had spent quite a lot of time talking to Fran and Vogel, or that Maria Lombardi, having run from the room, might have had access to another telephone somewhere else in the school building.

He started to light a cigarette, remembered that this was St. Catherine's, and decided to wait until he was outside. He went toward the door and was met by the woman who had first admitted him. Her eyes regarded him serenely. "You are leaving now?"

"Yes. Thank you for giving me a little time with Maria."

"I trust it was not bad news you brought her."

"Nothing that time won't heal," he said, and followed her to the front door. She opened it, smiled at him as he went out. The door closed gently.

Shannon went cautiously across the veranda, his caution being more instinct and habit than any actual suspicion of danger. In his talk with Big Nick Lombardi he had at no time allowed Lombardi to guess that the phone call had originated from this particular place. Therefore Lombardi had had no chance to trace him. Shannon looked across the grounds and saw nobody but the aged gardener. It was not until he, Shannon, had gone down the path and was completely through the wrought iron gates that he noticed the parked car on the opposite side of the street.

Sour-Puss, the ugly little hood who worked with Sticky, was leaning on the right front fender with a gun in his hand. He squeezed the trigger and Shannon's hat flew off. Shannon drew his own gun and shot the guy dead.

Down the street there was a tremendous racket and the hacker Osterwicz came wheeling furiously along the gutter, banked in a wide U-turn. "Get in!" he yelled.

Shannon got in. They went away from there.

It was a small house, on a street of small houses, yet there was a beauty in the street and a certain quiet dignity about the houses. These, you felt, were something a little more than mediocre five-room bungalows: they were homes. The people who lived here probably never worried the United States Treasury over income tax evasions, but they were a definite asset to the community. Late afternoon sunshine filtered through overhanging pepper trees.

Shannon got out of the cab at the farther corner, walked quietly down the side street and turned into an unpaved alley.

Little noises came to him from the kitchens of the houses he passed, the preparation of early suppers, no doubt, but no one came out to ask him his business. He halted at the little gate set into a shoulder-high hedge, looking at the tiny garden patch which his skipper had tended with his own hands. A few weeds had already begun to sprout, but the hands that had nurtured this garden would never return to do anything about it.

Shannon was very glad that Mrs. Grady had preceded her husband into the unknown.

Presently Shannon let himself through the gate and crossed the yard, more swiftly now, until he was hidden by the screened porch. It was so quiet here that the silence almost hurt his ears. The back door had been jimmied open. It swung loosely on its hinges as Shannon touched it.

He cursed bitterly, under his breath, and went into the kitchen. The place was a shambles. Even the flour and sugar and coffee canisters had been upended, dumped carelessly on the sink board and on the floor. Shannon made sibilant little sounds with his mouth. Anger made his broken arm throb.

In the living room, pictures hung awry on the walls, and some of them had even had their backs removed, the cardboard ripped off and the small brads yanked out. A twenty-year-old photograph of the skipper himself lay on the floor, face up, its protecting glass shattered by some vandal heel.

Shannon picked it up, looked at it. The eyes seemed slightly reproachful. Shannon said, "Hell, I'm still trying. You ought to know that." He shook the likeness. "You had something, guy. What was it? Where is it?"

There was only the mildly reproachful look in the pictured eyes to answer him.

He put the photograph on the table, sat down in a Morris chair almost denuded of upholstery like all the other chairs and the sofa in the room. It didn't seem particularly important to Shannon who had ravished the house, whether it was Big Nick Lombardi's hoods or Acting-Chief O'Meara's dicks. O'Meara could have done it, or had it done, for perfectly legitimate reasons. But regardless of who was responsible it was almost certain that the thing itself, whatever it was, had not been found. Or had it? Not by Lombardi, at least, Shannon concluded. Witness Lombardi's action in trying to force Shannon to help him get it.

Then there was the other thing that Lombardi had wanted, too. He'd wanted Shannon to turn up Floyd Duquesne for him.

Presuming that Lombardi had engineered the jail break for the purpose of clinching the skipper's murder on Duquesne, the plan had gone haywire. Duquesne had got away. Where was he now? What was his reason for ignoring his brother, Ward Duffield, the attorney? Shannon thought a little about the gray man with the club foot. For all his reputation and known sagacity, the lawyer had not been able to accomplish any more than Shannon had. It all seemed to hinge upon this unknown thing that had been in Captain Grady's possession. The whole case evolved from that.

Well, what was it? Evidence, surely. But evidence of what? And against whom? What were its ramifications, and how many would it have sent to prison—or to the cyanide squat at San Quentin? Last but far from least, did this evidence still exist or had it now been destroyed?

Captain Grady's killing had not been premeditated; of that Shannon was by this time almost positive. He reviewed the circumstances, analyzing them. The skipper's corpse had been found in an alley, with one exploded shell in his gun. Therefore you knew he had fired at the person who had shot him. But there was no assurance, merely because he had been found in the alley, that he had been killed there.

Any way you figured it, though, the framing of Floyd Duquesne was just a side play, an afterthought. There was no getting around the obvious fact that Duquesne had been a thorn in the side of Big Nick Lombardi; but he still hadn't been a big enough thorn to make necessary the skipper's murder.

It came to him, presently, that he still hadn't resolved the problem to its essentials. Who, he asked himself, stood to gain by the recent chain of events?

His Honor, Paul Shacklewood Argyle? Well, the killing of Captain Grady and the exposure of his venality—real or faked—certainly had not advanced the cause of the incumbent mayor. Rather, it had cast a cloud over the mayor's own reputation, because it was known that he and the skipper had been friendly.

Was Acting-Chief George O'Meara on Lombardi's side? Or was he operating independently, solely in the interest of George O'Meara? He was ruthlessly ambitious, so that you could answer this either way and it would make equal sense.

That brought the absent Chief Regan back into the picture. In a way, Shannon almost wished that Gus Vogel had been able to make telephone contact with Regan up in San Francisco this morning. At least Gus might have found out when Regan intended to come back to his desk. Maybe Regan, having made his morning speech at the convention was already on his way south. Or maybe he had decided to come home without making the speech at all. For that matter, perhaps he was going to stay out of town until the whole mess cleared. Shannon devoutly hoped not, although there was no telling how much good Regan could do even if he returned to his duties.

You could be certain of only one way in which Regan's presence would affect the situation. He would supercede O'Meara, at least temporarily; and O'Meara might not like this. He might like it so little, indeed, that he would take steps to see that Regan never did arrive. The same with Nick Lombardi.

Shannon frowned in thought. Floyd Duquesne was definitely involved. He was out to get the guy or guys who had framed him into a murder rap. And there, come to think about it, was another funny thing. Who had shot Boyer? Not Lombardi, surely. It would have been easier to shoot Shannon. Captain O'Meara, then? Well, why should he? Where was the motive? It was a crazy thing to do, and as Shannon thought of the word *crazy* he thought of a whitehaired woman in a quietly refined boarding house, and of her son, a bank teller named Frank Little.

He didn't know why he should have thought of them. Perhaps it was the kid's photograph, straight-looking eyes staring out of a sensitive face. That kind of kid might go off his nut, given the right provocation. Maybe he'd gotten loose from Lombardi; or maybe Lombardi had never picked him up. Maybe Floyd Duquesne had shot Boyer. He was another guy who had a good reason, although the method, the time and the place didn't seem to fit Duquesne.

Cursing half-heartedly, because he could just as well have done all this screw-pot reasoning in another place, and it certainly wasn't conducive to spirit-message reception, Shannon opened a closet door.

The guy inside the closet hit him with something so hard and so heavy that Shannon had only a blurred impression of the descending arm.

He went down like a poled ox.

Stunned, unable to see, he was still not so completely out that he couldn't feel it when the guy stepped on his chest. His flailing right fist closed on an ankle, closed hard, and he tried to get his eyes open so that he could see what he'd caught, but before he could manage this last the guy kicked him on the chin.

This time Shannon really went bye-bye. And when he woke up, a long time later, he was handcuffed to Chief Regan. Regan looked as though he might stay unconscious a whole lot longer than Shannon had.

At first Shannon was not aware that he was handcuffed to his chief of police. He realized only that he, Shannon, was stretched out on the floor and that Osterwicz, the hacker, was trying to unscrew his head from his shoulders. This was extremely painful indeed. Osterwicz sat astraddle Shannon's chest, one hand on either side of Shannon's jaw, and he was really working very hard at his rather unorthodox idea of resuscitation. Relief flooded his face as Shannon's eyes came open.

"Hot damn!" the hacker remarked. "Jesus, guy, I thought maybe you was dead!"

"You were certainly doing your best," Shannon grumbled. "Now would you mind getting off me, pal?"

"Not at all. Looks like your friend could use a little first aid, anyhow. I'll see what I can do." Osterwicz got off.

Shannon, not really hearing this remark, much less comprehending it, attempted to get up. Forgetting that he had only one good arm available, he tried to use both to pry himself off the floor and, as a result, fell flat on his back. Osterwicz, stooping, regarded him with grave concern. "You're in bad shape."

"Everybody has his moment of weakness. Shut up, you're bothering me."

"How many was there?"

"How many of what?"

"Hard guys that sapped you boys."

Shannon still didn't get the plural. "Just one."

"Only one? And the both of you let him take you like that? Pal, I'm beginning to lose my faith in you. Maybe it was an accident after all, your clunking me that time on account of my wife. Now look, chum, tell me straight. Who arrested who?"

Shannon closed his eyes. "Oh, quiet," he said. He was trying to think, but while thinking had been difficult enough before, now, with a head on him like a balloon, it was practically impossible. Without opening his eyes to look at Osterwicz, he said, "what the hell brought you in here so opportunely?"

"Well, I got tired of waiting for you, kind of, and so I just come in to find out what was delaying you." He clucked his tongue. "Boy, did I find out. This is the damndest thing I ever stumbled into. I think I better get busy on your fr—"

"You didn't see this party I was telling you about?"

"Party? What party?"

"The guy that brained me."

"Well, you ain't been telling me much about him, pal, and that's a fact. You just said he was one guy. What did he look like?"

"Let it pass," Shannon groaned, still keeping his eyes closed to vitiate the pain. "Let's just put it this way: Did you or did you not see anybody run out of this house?"

"I didn't see nobody run out and I didn't see nobody come in. I wasn't watching. I was reading a comic book. A new one, just out. Called Dan Turner, Hollywood Detective. Jesus, the jams that shamus can get hisself into. Almost as bad as you, pal."

"Well, I certainly couldn't ask for a more categorical answer than that," Shannon said. "Nor one more useless." Once more he attempted to sit up, this time being careful to use only his good arm. It was at this point that he first felt the handcuff on his wrist. Initially he thought it was merely his wrist watch. Then he remembered that he was wearing the wrist watch in his pocket. He opened his eyes, turned his head and yelled, "Well, for Christ's sake! Regan!"

Regan, manacled to him, lay supine, breathing stertorously. A little saliva dribbled from his flaccid lips. He didn't answer to his loudly shouted name.

Shannon came up on his haunches, shaking Regan's arm. He then turned wild eyes upon Osterwicz. "You bastard, how the hell did this happen?"

"That's what I was trying to ask you," the hackster's voice was indignant. "What I want to know is, who arrested who in this rassle? I happened to push his coat open, sort of, while I was bringing you around, and I seen he was wearing a badge pinned inside. So I figure he's a cop, and—"

"Of course he's a cop!" Shannon said through his teeth. "He's the chief of police!" He attempted awkwardly to massage the back of Regan's neck. "He's Vern Regan! Listen, you son of a bitch, if you pulled this handcuff trick on us I'll break every bone in your filthy little body!"

Osterwicz made a resentful mouth. "Is that a way to talk, pal? Me, I had an idea maybe he pinched you while you was frisking the joint, and nippered you to him so you wouldn't get away, and then you cold-cocked him and when he fell down he dragged you down with him and you bumped your head on the floor—"

Regan groaned a little.

"You halfwit!" Shannon raged at the hacker. "Why would Regan arrest me?"

"Well, ain't you wanted for the Boyer kill?" Osterwicz demanded with considerable logic. "And a chief of police is still a cop, no matter how you look at it. A chief can pinch guys the same as a harness bull, can't he?"

Regan blinked his eyes open. He had, apparently, been gradually regaining his senses for the past minute or two. In a thick and feeble voice he said, "A lot of nonsense."

"Regan, are you all right?" Shannon shook him.

"Don't know yet. Need a little time." He stirred. His eyes were wide open now. "God, my head!"

Shannon had a sudden thought. He looked at Osterwicz. "You got any whisky in your hack? If you haven't, go buy some and bring it. Fast."

Osterwicz went out. Regan was now blearily studying Shannon. He muttered, "Nonsense. You know I wouldn't handcuff you, Shannon. Guy must be out of his mind."

"Take it easy. We can talk when you're feeling better. When we both feel better," Shannon amended this, abruptly aware of the pain in his own skull.

"Talk now," Regan said. "I didn't handcuff you. I didn't arrest you."

"All right, I know it."

"Did you handcuff me, Shannon?" At sight of Shannon's face, Regan made instant apology. "Never mind, I'm sorry I asked. Naturally the answer is no. Don't get sore. My thinking is a little fuzzy."

"Mine too, but not that fuzzy."

Regan lifted his left arm, linked to Shannon's right. "Whose bracelets? Yours?"

"They can't be. I haven't been carrying mine since I changed clothes last night."

"Must be mine, then. Had them in my pocket."

Shannon said, "I wouldn't know. I don't know a goddamned thing about any of this. I was going through the house and opened a closet door and the roof caved in on me. This is the way I was when I came to."

"What were you doing here in the first place, Shannon?"

"Looking for something."

"Looking for what?"

"Object X, the unknown quantity. Whatever it was that Captain Grady had that made him dangerous to whoever killed him. I didn't find it. All I found was a clout on the head from a guy I didn't even see."

Regan said, "Same here." He drew a ragged breath. "We've got to talk about this, Shannon."

"Why don't we wait till Osterwicz brings us a drink? Then we'll feel more like comparing notes."

"Don't want to talk in front of anybody, Shannon. Don't trust anybody. Except you. I've got to trust you. I do trust you." Regan used his free hand to delve through his various pockets, produced a small shiny key. "Let's see if this works." He fitted it into the lock of the handcuffs and they fell open. "My cuffs, all right. So that proves one thing. Whoever slugged me is the same one that slugged you. He dragged me in here alongside you and fastened us together in case either of us revived and tried to stop his getaway. He used my handucffs to do it either because he had none of his own, or, if he had, he didn't want to leave them on us for fear he could be traced through them."

Shannon rotated his released wrist to restore the circulation. His hand felt a little numb. He didn't say anything.

"You see," Regan said, "I had the same idea you had. About Captain Grady's murder, I mean. Maybe Grady had evidence against somebody and was killed because of it. The killer framed Duquesne as an expedient. Grady's death might not have ended the danger to the killer, though. True, a dead man can't talk; but maybe he had left something tangible behind him, something which, if found, would blow the whole thing wide open. For that matter, that's why your car was bombed, to shut you up in case Grady had passed along his knowledge to you."

"Which he hadn't," Shannon said.

Regan nodded. "That's obvious. Otherwise you wouldn't have come here to his house, searching. I came for the same purpose."

"Did you tell anybody you were going to?"

"Christ, no! Do you think I'm a fool? I didn't even let anybody know I was leaving San Francisco. I didn't check out of the convention, I just booked plane passage under another name, right after I made my speech this morning. As far as I could tell, nobody that knows me saw me go aboard; nobody I recognized saw me disembark at Glendale. I even used one of the independent nonscheduled planes instead of an established airline. So then I came on out here to Grady's house and walked in, and bingo! My head hurts to beat all hell," he added grimly.

"So does mine. I think I'll live, though," Shannon said.

"That's the part I don't understand," Regan scowled. "As long as we were helpless, why were we allowed to live? Why didn't the guy knock us off the same as Grady was knocked off? Why just slug us and leave us to recover?"

Shannon got up, sank into a chair. "If we were dead, this unknown party would still be uncertain whether we had really known anything important—and whether we had passed the information to the D.A. The point is, he's gambling on being able to keep step with us. He's a hell of a bold gambler. He's playing his cards winner-take-all."

"Could be," Regan said, getting up on his feet. "Look, Shannon, what's been happening since I talked to you last night outside Argyle's office?"

Shannon inched himself out of the chair, headed for the bathroom. He talked as he went, with Regan following and listening. It didn't take long to acquaint the police chief with everything that had transpired since their hasty colloquy, many hours ago, in a City Hall corridor. True, a lot had happened, but Shannon made it terse, meanwhile dousing his face with cold water, toweling himself sketchily and running a comb through his pepper-and-salt hair.

He turned to Regan. "You said one thing that interests me. It was about the handcuffs. You said whoever slugged us used your cuffs either because he had none of his own or, if he had, he didn't want to risk being traced through them. That seems to mean you suspect a cop. What cop?"

"I don't know, Shannon. I could be all wrong about it."

"O'Meara?"

"Possibly. Or again, possibly not." Regan peered at himself in the glass. "I look like the wrath of God. Feel like it, too." He eyed Shannon. "If it was O'Meara, or anybody else from Headquarters, the word will soon be out that I'm back in town. If the word doesn't get out—"

"It won't mean anything except that whoever sapped us is keeping quiet about it," Shannon shrugged. "And it strikes me you'd better keep quiet about it too. If you want to do undercover work, stay under cover. Operating separately, you and I can accomplish one thing at least; we'll force our unknown friend to try to watch in two directions at one, which won't be so easy."

"Good idea, Shannon. Perhaps I'd better slip out of here now. Incidentally, what about your hacker? You told him who I am. Is he likely to spill it?"

Shannon's face darkened. "Not if he wants to stay healthy."

"Well, I'll see you, Shannon. I'll find a way to contact you, later on. And if circumstances force my hand I'll walk into Headquarters and take over from O'Meara." Regan went out the back door, very quietly.

A moment later, Osterwicz came in the front. He had a pint of bourbon. He put startled eyes on Shannon and said,

"For God's sake, are you Houdini or something? Where's your pal?"

"Pal? What pal?"

"The guy you was handcuffed to. The chief of police."

Shannon snatched the bottle, uncorked it. "You must be out of your mind. What have you been smoking, opium?" He let a long drink go down his throat. "I wasn't handcuffed to anybody, and if you so much as mention it again I'll break off your legs and beat you over the head with them. That's a promise."

"Well, Jesus! Like that, hunh?"

"Like that. Here, have a drink." Osterwicz had a drink. Shannon had another. He began to feel better. He discovered that he still had his gun, which astonished and pleased him. Getting sapped had wounded his pride as well as his head, but finding that the guy neglected to disarm him afterward served to restore a modicum of his self respect, even though he recognized that the reasoning behind this was a little specious.

Osterwicz, refreshed no end by the contents of the bottle, announced happily that he was ready to go if Shannon was.

They went out and got in the cab. "Where to, pal?"

Shannon gave him the address of Frank Little, the bank teller. They drove out there. Traffic had thickened, three lanes outbound, only one inbound. Lights were beginning to come on in the stores, though it was by no means completely dark. Shannon's watch pointed to five-thirty.

Turning right from the crush of the boulevard into the quiet backwater of the Little's street Shannon cursed suddenly. There was a car parked halfway down the block. Not that there weren't other cars too, but this one stood out to the eyes of an experienced copper. For one thing, there aren't many touring cars being driven any more. Those that are don't usually have their curtains up in dry weather.

Shannon said, "Take it easy, but don't stop. Go on around the block."

He slid deep into his seat, eyes just above the sill of the quarter-window. There were three men in the touring car. One of them was the saturnine Sticky, the gun who worked for Nick Lombardi and who wanted some day to horse a plane around the sky.

CHAPTER EIGHT

THERE WASN'T MUCH DOUBT about which house Sticky and his two companions were watching. Shannon, in fact, had no doubts about it whatever. "Keep going," he said.

"Trouble, hunh?"

"Not if I can avoid it."

On the next block Shannon found that the two streets and the boulevard made a sort of triangle, narrowing down to a point where it was no longer possible to get two full-depth lots back to back. The Little lot ran clear through, although there was no rear entrance. The garages were flanked by a lattice-work trellis, rank with rambler roses.

Shannon had to get Osterwicz to help him spring one edge of the trellis free, so that he could squeeze through. He crossed the lot to the back porch, nibbling at a rose thorn in his thumb.

Martha, the maid, opened the back door to his knock. Immediately she recognized Shannon she tried to shut him out. He stuck his foot in the opening. "So he's here, eh, Martha?"

"Who?" Her ebony face had turned the color of putty. She started a scream as she saw Shannon was coming in, choked it off when he grabbed her arm.

"Don't do it, Martha," he advised. "Maybe you and his mother don't want him pinched, but believe me a pinch is better than a gunning. That's what he'll get if you scare him out the front door."

Her eyes rolled up in her head till only the whites showed. Shannon saw she had fainted and let her drop. He went quietly up the hall and began climbing the stairs. Somewhere above him a woman sobbed quietly. He followed the sound to an open bedroom door.

It was Frank Little's room.

He just stood there in the doorway for a moment. For the first time in his life he felt the need of someone, Frances McGowan preferably.

In his time he had dragged plenty of sons away from their mothers, but in most cases the sons had been rats and the mothers not much better. This pair was different. They had breeding and education, and for people like that the going was always tougher. The kid was in a chair, his mother on her knees beside him, trying to bandage his arm and not making a very good job of it because she was crying and couldn't see very well. There was blood all over the kid's shirt, which lay on the floor.

Shannon went in. "Don't get up, Mrs. Little."

She sat perfectly still, not even turning her head. The kid stared at Shannon over her bowed shoulder. "Who are you?"

"Name of Shannon, son. I'm a cop. I was here before, only you weren't in. You were downtown, shooting a guy that no doubt needed shooting, but it made it a little tough on me. So I came back."

The kid ran a tongue over dry lips. "How do you know?"

Shannon let his eyes rest on the bloody shirt. "I suspect it was my slug that potted you, there on the fire escape. Funny how things work out, isn't it?"

Mrs. Little got slowly to her feet. "Funny! Do you call it funny when—when a city is so corrupt that things like this can happen to decent people?" She pointed a finger at Shannon. "It's your kind that makes these things possible; that permits gambling and vice to flourish. Is it his fault that he's where he is?" She covered her face suddenly. "Oh, my God!"

Shannon touched her gently.

"Police departments are just like any other group of men, ma'am. Putting a uniform on a guy, or giving him a badge, don't change him inside. I wish it did just as much as you do, but it don't. So all we can do is make the best of things as they are."

There was more of it; quite a lot. His voice droned on and on and presently it had its effect. The woman quieted.

The kid looked helplessly at his mother, looked without a great deal of resentment at Shannon. "You—you said 'make the best of things as they are.' I'd like to make it easier for mother, is all."

"So would I," Shannon said sincerely. He went over and stood the kid on his feet. "I can't promise you much, but if you and your mother will go down to the end of the hall I'll show you what I mean by making the best of things."

They went down the unlighted hall to a window overlooking the street. "There's a car out there," Shannon said. "A black phaeton with three men in it. Even if I were a cop in good standing I couldn't do much to them for just sitting there, but you know and I know what they're there for. They can't make up their minds whether you're home or not. After a while they may decide to come in after you. I'm offering you a better chance than that."

Mrs. Little drew an audible breath. "Is there a chance that—that if Frank goes with you, something can be done about things like that?"

Shannon inclined his head. "A good chance, ma'am. Frank will probably have to take a rap of some kind, but even that is better than being found in a gutter some place. I can get him Ward Duffield as counsel, and if he tells a straight story he'll get all the breaks possible. I can't promise more."

She looked at him. "You—you don't bear my son any malice for what he did you to? I mean—"

"That I'm accused of the killing that he did?" Shannon laughed shortly. "Hell, ma'am, we all do screwy things at one time or another."

The three of them went back to the kid's room. Shannon hadn't taken his gun out once during the interview. No gun was needed to escort the kid from the house by the back door and across the rear yard and through the trellis to Osterwicz in his waiting cab. Thirty minutes later Shannon had Little at Headquarters, and at no time had the slightest show of force been necessary.

Captain O'Meara was in Chief Regan's office. He was sitting at Regan's desk as though this had become permanently his, and his captain's uniform shone from a recent pressing. His olive face looked tired, though.

Shannon and Frank Little sat in chairs facing the desk, each with an arm in a sling, otherwise totally unlike. Ward Duffield's club foot made little clumping sounds on the floor as he roved about the big room. Jack Runyon of the *Telegram* sat on a leather couch and smoked incessantly. The presence of Runyon and Duffield was Shannon's idea.

O'Meara toyed with the leaden pellet they had taken out of the kid's arm. Shannon's gun, the one he had dropped in Tex Boyer's office, also lay on the desk. It had been fired only once.

Shannon looked at the kid. "Tell it, son. Tell it in your own words, so they won't think I've coached you."

O'Meara said, "That wasn't necessary, Shannon. The slug and the gun just about clear you. I couldn't do anything about it even if I wanted to."

Shannon flushed uncomfortably. A lot of this had been his own fault, but, being Shannon, he hated to admit it. Besides, he still wasn't sure of O'Meara. The guy hadn't switched the slugs in the Captain Grady kill; perhaps he'd been acting in good faith, arresting Floyd Duquesne. But there was no assurance that he wasn't taking Lombardi's money for other things.

The kid began in a low voice, "Tex Boyer had me in a spot. He was into me for more than two thousand dollars, money he knew I couldn't have saved out of my salary. He began pressing me and finally I had to tell him the money was coming out of the bank. I was pretty desperate. When he had me on the ragged edge he threatened to suggest an investigation at the bank."

Ward Duffield said, "You don't have to tell this, you know."

"That's *your* story!" Shannon said. "Go on, kid."

The boy went on: "Boyer wanted me to get hold of one of Duquesne's checks. He said it was to be used to run Duquesne out of business. He didn't tell me about—about killing anybody. So I got the check, called him and he came down and left cash in exchange for the check. Five thousand dollars in currency."

"Just a minute," O'Meara interrupted. "As I understand it, all your dealings were with Boyer? You saw nothing of Big Nick Lombardi?"

"No."

Shannon yelled, "We all know the big guy was behind Boyer!"

O'Meara gave him a level stare. "Knowing it and proving it are two different things, Shannon. One thing you did succeed in doing—you busted the Ticker Club out into the open. But Lombardi only shows as the owner of the building. I doubt if we could hang him for that."

Shannon shut his lips on a hot retort. "Go ahead, kid."

The boy's mouth twisted in a bitter grimace. "I was a sap. Boyer promised to square me at the bank and I believed him. Instead of squaring me he gave me a hundred dollars and told me I'd better leave town. Well, I almost went screwy right then, but he finally convinced me there was nothing I could do. I couldn't prove he had got the Duquesne check without admitting I was a party to it. Maybe not even then.

"My shortage was bound to show up pretty soon, even if he didn't drop the hint he threatened. I told him I'd lam. But I didn't. I hung on for a few days more, hoping something would turn up. Then I saw where that—that police captain had been killed, and what the check had been used for, and I guess I went off my nut. I couldn't think of anything but getting Boyer.

"I walked the streets all last night and most of the morning. Finally I remembered the fire escape outside his office. I had a gun, because I'd thought once of committing suicide. I went up to his window. It was open, and there he was with his back so close I could almost touch him. I could hear him talking to somebody, I didn't know who.

"All I knew was that he was there, right under my gun, and I blamed him for everything that had happened. I shot him." He sagged in his chair, closing his eyes. You knew he was glad it was all over at last.

O'Meara looked at Shannon. "All right, your slug went through the slit in the drapes and plugged the kid. Then what? Why'd he go home? How did you know it was him?"

"I just thought it might be," Shannon said. "I tried to pin it on Lombardi, on you, even on Duquesne. It seemed to me that any one of you, even if you had a motive, would have more sense than to go up that fire escape in broad daylight. At first I thought Lombardi"—he paused, staring at O'Meara—"well, if you don't like Lombardi's name in this let's just call him 'somebody.' I thought that *somebody* would have taken the kid for a ride by this time.

"Then I thought that maybe they hadn't, or maybe he'd got away like Floyd Duquesne did. I'd seen the kid's room, seen his picture, and he looked like the kind that breaks under pressure. And after he'd broken I figured he'd need his mother. So I went up."

Jack Runyon leaped to his feet. "That was damned smart work, Shannon!"

"Well," Shannon said, "it was smarter work than you or Vogel or O'Meara did. You let one of Lombardi's"—

again he looked at Acting Chief O'Meara—"pardon me, one of Boyer's hired help to get away with the spent slug that went clear through Boyer."

O'Meara put his hard eyes on Shannon. "You've got a goddamned nasty streak in you somewhere, Irish. You've thrown a lot of innuendos around—yes, and a lot of direct accusations. Before witnesses I'm willing to admit that I've made mistakes. You're in the clear on Boyer's murder. You can have your badge back if you want it. But I can't have you running around shooting off your mouth and making me out a son of a bitch. I *won't* have it."

Shannon got up and leaned on the desk. He was a fool and he knew it, but he had a stubborn streak in him. "You can keep the lousy badge, O'Meara. I'm still looking for the guy that killed my skipper." He pushed his broken arm out in front of him. "Yes, and the guy that gave me this."

"You haven't submitted anything to prove that it wasn't Floyd Duquesne."

"The skipper, maybe," Shannon said. "Not the arm. Duquesne was in jail at the time, if you remember. Or had you forgotten all about that?"

O'Meara reddened. "Then who else?"

"For a guess," Shannon said, "I give you Big Nick Lombardi." He didn't really think this any more. He was just baiting O'Meara into some kind of action that would definitely prove or disprove him Lombardi's man. He looked at Ward Duffield. "Do what you can for the kid, will you? His story itself ought to be almost enough, don't you think?"

Duffield nodded. "I've had worse cases."

"Yes, and beaten them!" Jack Runyon chortled. "Boy, oh, boy, let me at that door!" He clattered out.

Gus Vogel waddled in on the echo of the newspaper reporter's hasty departure. He took off his derby, peered in it, didn't find anything and looked at Shannon. "Hello, John J. I hear you ain't a murderer no more.

"I've reformed."

Vogel's eyes widened in surprise. "Is that a fact!"

Shannon stared at O'Meara, looked at Duffield, finally went over and laid his good hand gently on Frank Little's shoulder. "Take a brace, fella. I'll be seeing you." He then took Gus Vogel by the arm and led him out into the corridor. "What did you do with the dame?"

"Miss McGowan, you mean?"

"Who else, stupid?"

Vogel fidgeted. "Well, now, Miss McGowan is in jail."

"The hell she is! What for?"

"Well, now, look, you told me to put her in a safe place, didn't you? There ain't no safer place than jail, is there?"

"Of all the crazy God damned—" Shannon broke off, suddenly laughed. "You're priceless, you Dutch bastard. I don't know what I'd do without you. I could try, though." He turned and made for the elevator. Vogel panted along in his wake.

Frances was in one of the nice shiny new detention cells over in the women's wing. She was working on a hooked rug begun by a former inmate. Shannon peered at her through the bars. "What are you in for, pal?"

"I'm not quite sure I think I'm a vag." She went on poking yarn through the stretched burlap. The matron looked disapprovingly from Gus Vogel to Shannon.

Shannon said ingratiatingly, "You hungry, pal?"

"I could eat."

"Then let's all eat," Shannon suggested. He looked at the matron. "Send out for some steaks and things, hunh, Jeep? Charge it to our friend Vogel here."

Vogel poked a plump finger through the bars. "You mean eat in there, John J.?"

"Where else? If it's safe for Miss McGowan it's safe for us, isn't it? Besides, we've got to question the prisoner." Shannon stood aside for the matron to unlock the door. They went inside. Jeep went away, presumably to send out for the steaks and things.

Frances stood up. "I've stood a lot from you, John J. Shannon, but never anything like this!"

"Now look, kitten, was it my idea? Didn't I tell Gus to see you to a nice safe place? Is it my fault if he's too literal? Not," he added, "that our jails are the safest places in the world, lately. Look at Duquesne."

Frances suddenly buried her face against his chest. "Oh, Shan, I've been worried to death about you! What's happened?"

Shannon told her everything. He didn't make a production of it but he didn't omit anything, either.

Vogel clucked in dismay. "You mean you'd have actually shot Lombardi's kid?"

Shannon's eyes had a hard, reckless light in them. "You're God damned right I would have." He hesitated. "I think."

Fran said, "Liar. What I want to know is, if you hadn't had a broken arm and a lot of other things on your mind, would you have gone for that Karen redhead?"

"There's no doubt of it."

Vogel's round face had a shocked expression. "I don't believe it."

"Well, wouldn't you have if you'd been in my shoes?"

Fran giggled. "Of course he would have. Gus is a wolf. Pay no attention to his sheep's clothing."

Fran had just finished an account of her kidnapping by Lombardi's hoods when Jeep, the matron, pushed a loaded mobile tray through the door. "This is very unusual, I must say."

"But isn't it cozy?" Frances jeered. "Like the bear pit in the zoo." She attacked her steak.

After a while the matron came back leading Ward Duffield. Shannon got up, wiping his mouth, and went close to the bars. He kept his voice down to a whisper. "You hear any more from Floyd?"

"Not a word," the gray man said. "I'm beginning to wonder if Lombardi—"

"Lombardi hasn't got him. At least he didn't have when I was up there. Lombardi wanted me to finger him."

"Would you have?"

Shannon nodded. "I think so. I'm not sure."

"Nothing like honesty, is there, Shannon?"

"Lombardi had my girl. If necessary, I'd have made any bargain he forced on me. Luckily I found another way out."

Duffield smiled, thinly. "You seem to be expert at finding ways out. I hope you can keep it up." He gave Shannon a keen glance and asked, "Any word from Regan?"

"I haven't even had time to read the speech he made at the convention," Shannon's answer, while true, was actually no answer at all. He watched Duffield limp away on his club foot, then turned and finished up his meal.

When Jeep came to wheel away the dishes, Shannon went with them. He felt pretty good.

Presently he felt even better. He stood in an ell of the great stone steps leading up to City Hall and shook out a limp copy of the *Telegram.* He often marveled at the speed with which news hit the streets, and this present occasion was no exception. Shannon himself had made the headlines this time. He was exonerated of the killing of Tex Boyer and would probably be reinstated as a lieutenant of detectives, the result of his praiseworthy efforts at solving that murder. The corners of Shannon's mouth quirked as he read Jack Runyon's somewhat hectic account of how he, Shanno, had persuaded Frank Little to confess the shooting.

There was no mention in the newspaper of Nick Lombardi. You felt that Lombardi was apparently just one of those unfortunate landlords whose tenants turned out to be undesirable. Death and a police raid had simply served as a form of eviction.

Shannon thought about the missing Floyd Duquesne, frowned and crumpled the paper, threw it away. He went into the domed foyer of City Hall and shut himself up in a phone booth.

He spent considerable time and money calling different bus stations, railroad terminals and airports, local and long distance. When he came out of the phone booth he was sweating. He went up to the mayor's office.

There was quite a crowd around, the same as last night, though Big Nick Lombardi and Sticky and Sour-Puss were conspicuously absent. Sour-Puss, indeed, would probably be absent for a long time to come, Shannon having shot him cold that afternoon in front of St. Catherine's School.

Seven stenographers were busy pounding out Mayor Argyle's last pre-election speech. Shannon looked over the shoulder of one of them. "Pap!" he sneered. The harried-looking blonde secretary popped out of the mayor's door. "Please don't interrupt the girl!" she snapped. Then, recognizing Shannon: "Oh, it's you!"

"Up jumper the devil," Shannon grinned. He jerked his head toward the closed door. "You want to announce me or shall I just walk in?"

Angry color flooded her face. "His Honor is very busy. He goes on the air in half an hour." She took a bunched sheaf of manuscript from one of the seven girls. Shannon relieved her of it. "I'll give it to him." He opened the door, banged it closed behind him, leaned his back against it.

Argyle, busy rehearsing script at his too-big desk, looked up, startled. "Oh, hello, Shannon."

Shannon looked down at the typewritten sheets in his hand. He said, "You're intending to make this speech tonight?"

"Certainly."

"It'll be your political death knell. I told you I was going to smash this town wide open. I'm all set to do it. Tonight, the way it stacks up now. If you've aligned yourself with Lombardi you'll go down when he does. If you aren't aligned with him, this wishy-washy stuff, this sheepdip, will pull you down anyway."

"Now, see here!"

"Don't you know when you're sitting on a volcano? Can't you understand that now is the time to come out with some good strong red meat for the voters to sink their teeth in? Tear this thing up and tell the world you aren't Lombardi's man, or anybody's man save your own. Tell 'em you're going to reorganize the police department. Tell 'em anything, but make it strong—and mean it!"

"Reorganize the police department? Good God, I couldn't do a thing like that to Regan. Not until he gets here and I have a talk with him. If he wants to make changes it should be his prerogative. After all, he's the chief; I don't want to interfere behind his back. Besides, he's due in on the ten o'clock plane. I owe him the courtesy of a conference, at least."

"You've heard from him?" Shannon concealed any surprise he may have felt. "He's definitely coming?"

"Yes. And until I see him I don't want to upset anything. You know O'Meara might try to make capital of it."

O'Meara!" Shannon said sourly. Then, "I hope this doesn't mean you've thrown in with Lombardi."

The mayor flushed. "Lombardi could break me if you've guessed wrong, Shannon."

"But I'm not guessing wrong!" Shannon yelled. He brandished the sheaf of manuscript. "Look, let me tear this damned thing up and give you a good speech. Then I'll go see Lombardi. I want to see his face anyway when he hears you."

Argyle said quietly, "I'm listening, Shannon." He listened for fifteen minutes straight. When Shannon finally ran out of breath the mayor stood up. "I'll do it. By God, I'll do it!"

Shannon mopped sweat from his forehead. "I think I should have been a lawyer." He jammed on his hat, went out the side door, descended to the street and looked around for Osterwicz.

The hacker was munching stolidly on a sandwich. "Where you been, pal?"

"I'm in the laundry business now," Shannon told him. "I've been putting a little starch in a guy's backbone. I hope it don't make him so brittle he breaks himself." Under his breath he added, "And me."

He made a little prayer, because, while he wouldn't have admitted it to anybody but himself, he was doing a lot of guessing, and, as Mayor Argyle had said, the guessing might be wrong. Shannon nudged his thought aside, got in the cab. He was grateful that Vern Regan had finally decided to return to town officially; that would be a help. Regan was being smart about it. No doubt he had caught a plane north as far as, say, Ventura, and would there board the south-bound liner from which he would make his grand entrance, automatically demoting Acting-Chief O'Meara back to a captaincy. Shannon decided that things would really hum, then.

He spoke to Osterwicz. "Let's go see Nick Lombardi."

CHAPTER NINE

GOING INTO THE APARTMENT lobby Shannon saw only five or six casuals. They might be Lombardi's men, they might not. He went directly to the desk. "Get Lombardi on the wire for me."

Presently he heard the big guy's liquid-velvet voice. "Hello, Shannon."

"The eyes and ears of the world again," Shannon grumbled. "Damned if I know how you do it, but maybe we'll take this place apart some day and find out." He hesitated a moment before he said, "I've got something for you." Lombardi might already have the thing he had bargained with Shannon for. Besides, he no longer had Fran McGowan. There was a chance the big guy might figure Shannon as out for dough, though. In case he didn't have the stuff. Shannon held his breath.

"Come on up, Shannon," the velvet voice invited.

Shannon crossed the lobby to the elevator, got in. No one offered to stop him, no one tried to get in with him. The control was in automatic position. Shannon jabbed the top-floor button, went up. He stepped out of the car when it drifted to its purring stop and its door whispered open.

The two guys sitting on either side of Lombardi's door had guns in their laps. They stood up without hurry, closed in on Shannon, patted all of his pockets and peeled back his coat, felt for an armpit clip. They lifted his broken arm out of the way, somewhat roughly, and felt behind that. They searched the sling and cast itself, ran their hands down his pants legs. They didn't find anything.

Shannon's grin was jeering. "You might at least help me get it back in the sling," he said mildly. One of them did this, ungraciously, and the other opened the door.

Shannon went in.

Big Nick Lombardi was apparently all alone.

Shannon looked around with elaborate concern. "What," he said, "no Sticky?"

"Sticky is a very busy man," Lombardi smiled. "In a way he is quite sensitive, too. He feels very badly about what you did to his pal."

"Poor old Sour-Puss," Shannon sighed.

Lombardi moved a little among his cushions. Magically there was a gun in his fat hand and he looked at Shannon sleepy-eyed. "No," he shook his head, "poor old Shannon." He fondled the gun. "What you did to Maria today I cannot forgive, Mr. Shannon."

"I didn't do anything to her."

"You frightened her."

"I frightened you, you mean. Maria don't scare easily. She's a cool customer to be such a hot number."

"God damn you, Shannon—"

"Now look," Shannon said. "I thought we agreed that the two girls canceled each other out. Sauce for the goose, eh?" He laughed a little wildly.

Lombardi didn't laugh. "It is you who are the goose, Shannon. You walk in here without a gun. Nick Lombardi has one, no?" He sat erect suddenly, swung thick legs around so that his feet rested on the rug. "You will not walk out, I think. You will be carried out."

"You'd shoot me down just like that, hunh?"

"Just like that," Lombardi agreed. "Men do not play games with Lombardi's girl and live."

"You played games with mine."

Lombardi smiled then. "Ah, but you do not have a gun and I have. That is the difference." He broke off, listening to the radio. The mayor was being introduced.

Shannon led one of his two aces. "You wanted some evidence, Nick. Stuff that Captain Grady had. You still want it?"

"Meaning you have it?" Lombardi's eyes were suddenly alert and filled with suspicion. Shannon knew then that he had guessed right.

"I can get it."

The big guy's smile came back. "Then if you can get it we'll have no trouble finding it—after you're gone." He listened to Mayor Argyle. Quite suddenly his face went white and flaccid, and his eyes became mere pinpoints in the rolls of flesh. The eyes settled definitely on Shannon's face. "So—you know!"

"Yes," Shannon said, "I know."

Lombardi's trigger finger contracted.

Shannon overturned a table in the path of the first slug, dropped to the floor as two more slugs spatted into the heavy mahogany. Echoes boomed and billowed around the room.

Shannon got his own gun from where he had hidden it in his hat, jackknifed out from behind the table and put two quick slugs into Lombardi's chest.

Lombardi slid off the chaise longue, a sodden mass of flesh, inert. Foam bloodied his mouth, but his eyes still lived, he still clutched the gun. On his belly, he jacked his gun wrist up with his left hand.

Shannon kicked at him just as the door crashed in. Lombardi's slug dropped one of his own hoods instead of Shannon. Shannon shot the other one. Lombardi died. The beautiful room no longer smelled of lilac vegetal. It smelled of cordite. It was as though the big guy, dying, had taken all the perfume in the world with him.

Paul Shacklewood Argyle's radio speech ended. "Lombardi must go!" The mayor didn't know that Lombardi had already gone.

Shannon got out of there. Nobody got in his way. He was glad the path was clear; his stomach was tied in a tight knot and another killing would probably have brought on active nausea. He wondered if Maria would go merrily to hell, now that she no longer had a father to stop her. He didn't care, much. He did hope, though, that Karen Kane would find somebody else to keep her in mink coats. She would probably miss Lombardi more than Maria would.

Using the stairway instead of the elevator, because an elevator could easily become a trap, Shannon went down to the street. Osterwicz was waiting for him. "Have any trouble, pal?"

"Some."

Osterwicz held the cab door open for him. "You been smoking a new brand of cigarettes? Smells more like gunpowder than tobacco."

"Somebody set off a firecracker," Shannon said. He settled into the back seat. "Get up there and drive. Pretty soon this isn't going to be a healthy neighborhood at all."

Shannon was about thirty seconds too late to stop the thing. Maybe he couldn't have stopped it anyway. He hadn't anticipated such a crowd at the airport, hadn't realized that the mayor's radio speech, threatening to clear up the police department would send a mob out to see the man who headed that department, when he came in.

The administration building was jammed. So were the steps outside giving on the ramp, and the long promenade.

Shannon was at the port in time to hear the big ship come in but the crowd slowed him. He was still on the steps, looking down at the exit from the field when he saw Floyd Duquesne. Duquesne was hatless, easily recognizable even in a crowd, because of his height.

Shannon started plowing through a sea of softly resistant bodies. He was less than ten feet away when he saw Sticky, Lombardi's gunman, between him and Duquesne. Then everything seemed to happen at once.

It was perfectly clear when you had all the actors spotted, like a slow-motion picture, or a dream in which you can see what's going on with crystal clarity, but are powerless to interfere because of paralysis.

Chief Regan descended from the plane with a bulging suitcase in his hand. Floyd Duquesne's hand came out of the crowd with a gun in it. There was a little puff of smoke from the gun muzzle. Chief Regan staggered, went down.

Sticky shot Duquesne in the back of the head.

Shannon's breath sobbed in his throat as he hurled himself into the crush. Gun out, eyes hot with anger, belly churning, he met Sticky chest to chest. He shot Sticky three times in the stomach, once in the throat before he actually knew he had done it.

Another gun sounded. A slug glanced off the cast on Shannon's broken arm, nicking the plaster a little and whining into a wall. People fell away from Shannon like an ebb tide flowing out through a figure. The screaming of women made the night hideous. Shannon ran out onto the field where men bent over Chief Regan. Sirens added their din to the screaming of the women. Regan climbed shakily to his feet.

Shannon yelled "Where you hit?"

Regan recognized him. "Hello boy. I'm not hit any place."

"Huh?"

Regan shook his head. "Fact. It was the suitcase that got it. Knocked me off my pins and I bumped my head." He grinned at the plane crew. "Thanks a lot, anyway." He took Shannon's arm and they walked toward the exit. A flock of harness bulls were beating the crowd back. The chief's voice was no longer genially heroic for the benefit of interested listeners as he growled, "Did you see who the son of a bitch was, Shannon?"

Shannon nodded. "Floyd Duquesne."

"Duquesne! But why?"

"Maybe he didn't like you," Shannon offered.

Regan looked at Shannon's gun. "You get him?"

"Another guy got him first. I got the other guy. Someone else tried for me, too, but missed. Took a little plaster off my cast." Shannon shoved the gun in his pocket. It cost them ten minutes to explain all this to the harness bulls. Then they went out and got in a cab. Osterwicz had his hack in the line but Shannon pretended not to see him. Osterwicz started to yell resentfully at this obviously intentional slight, but then he caught Shannon's warning expression and subsided. Shannon muttered to Regan, "He knows better than to let on you were in town today, but no use taking any chances. If we rode with him he might want to get gabby. I can always make it up to him later, after you decide whether or not you want people to know your comings and goings."

"Okay, Shannon. Not that my comings and goings did me a hell of a lot of good." Regan frowned. "I'm sorry I wasn't able to get in touch with you sooner but I guess you were moving around too much; anyhow I couldn't seem to reach you. What did you find out, if anything?"

Before Shannon could answer, Runyon of the *Telegram* came pelting to their cab and stuck his head in. "Hi, Chief. Hello, Shannon. Going to Headquarters? Mind if I ride down with you?" Not waiting to be invited, he piled in.

Regan said, "No statement, fella. When I have anything to say to the press I'll tell all you boys together."

"So all you get is a free ride downtown," Shannon said. "Let's go, driver."

They went down to Headquarters.

Captain O'Meara was in Chief Regan's office. So was Mayor Argyle. It looked as though they'd been having a hot session. A little shamefacedly, O'Meara got out of Regan's chair. "Hello, Regan. Have a nice trip?"

"Just fine," Regan said. He was genial again. "Fine." He rubbed his hands together, looking beamingly at Shannon. "Even the end of it was exciting, wasn't it, boy?"

"That wasn't the end," Shannon said. "This is." He hit Regan in the mouth. Regan fell against the desk, didn't go all the way down. He took out a handkerchief, dabbed at his cut lip. Then, very deliberately, he went around the desk and sat down in his chair. His agate-hard eyes drilled O'Mearo. "You put him up to this?"

O'Meara said, "No." He didn't say anything else.

Mayor Argyle's glasses glinted frostily. "You left out this part, Shannon."

"I thought he might be listening to you on the air. They have radios in airplanes too, these days. He might have decided to bail out."

Chief Regan pressed all the buttons on his desk at once. Outside, an alarm gong sounded. At least forty cops tried to come through the door in a bunch. Regan pointed a finger at Shannon. "Arrest that man."

Argyle said pettishly, "Go away."

Captain O'Meara didn't say anything, just stood there.

Shannon reached across the desk and struck Regan in the mouth again. Nobody did anything for about a minute. Mayor Argyle took off his glasses, pointed them at the cops in the door. "I said to go away."

They decided that, afterall, he was mayor of the city. They went away.

Regan began yelling. "What is this? A frame, hunh? You lousy bastards you've jobbed me, the lot of you!" He didn't get out of his chair.

Across the room, Jack Runyon, white-faced, was inching toward a telephone. Shannon saw him out of the tail of his eye. "Stay away from it, buster. I'll let you know when I want you to make a move."

Runyon sat down.

Mayor Argyle looked at Shannon. "I'm still trusting you, but this is all over my head. Hadn't we better clear it up before the rest of the reporters come trooping in here?"

Shannon's eyes glowed. "Regan shot my skipper. He shot a guy who had been his friend for twenty years. I'm reserving a front row seat to see him gassed for it."

"You'll never see it," Regan said, "because I didn't do it. I was in San Francisco when it happened."

Shannon looked at him. "You were not in San Francisco when it happened, you were here. You went north to the convention, flew south again for the kill. The skipper gave you all the breaks a friend could, but you weren't satisfied. You wanted to hang onto your office and the side money. There was no way you could do this with the skipper alive, because he was honest. So you sneaked back and shot him."

"You're a God damned fool!"

"Sure. I've never claimed to be anything else. That's why it took me so long to get the picture." Shannon started unstrapping Regan's suitcase.

Regan took a gun from his waistband. "Leave it alone, Shannon. Hands off."

"I was waiting for that," Shannon said. "That's why I wouldn't let you ride in Osterwicz's cab just now. He knew you'd been back in town this afternoon, your third time south, incidentally, and you might have plugged him to keep him from spilling. Just as you would have plugged me during the excitement at the airport, only you merely nicked my cast. That's why I let Runyon ride downtown with us so you wouldn't try again. He sort of cramped your style."

"You son of a bitch." Regan's gun-hand jerked.

Shannon hurled himself straight at the gun as it went off. The slug went through the plaster cast and the splints, through the broken arm, only a little way into his chest. It didn't stop him. It didn't even slow him.

Before Regan could squeeze the trigger a second time Shannon's fist closed on the gun, wrenched it free. He began beating Regan over the head with it, quite methodically. O'Meara and Argyle managed, finally, to pull him off.

"Shannon, you're crazy!"

He looked down at the gun in his hand. "A little," he admitted. He smiled then, looking at Regan's head. "It's nice to be crazy once in a while. He bruises easily, doesn't he?"

The gun fell out of his hand and he sat down suddenly. Runyon came over and put a hand on his shoulder.

O'Meara got down on his knees beside Regan. Presently he rose, staring moodily at Shannon. "You didn't kill him."

"I tried." Shannon looked at Regan's ankles. On one of them, through the sheer silk, you could see black and blue marks, as if very strong fingers had gripped the ankle quite recently. "Yes, he bruises easily," Shannon said. "I put those marks on him this afternoon, in Captain Grady's house. He was there ahead of me looking for something he hadn't yet found. I walked in and he hid in a closet, sapped me when I opened the closet door. He didn't want to kill me then because he had to ask me a question; he wanted to know if I'd found the thing he was hunting. So he pretended that whoever sapped me also slugged him. He worked a handcuff trick to win my confidence. I was dumb enough to fall for it. We left the house—separately. He probably went back to the house later and found what he wanted. From then on he intended to kill me and probably Osterwicz too, so we could never testify he'd been back in town. Things happened at the airport that made him miss me. After that I managed to copper all his bets."

Argyle said, "What was he looking for?"

"You might search his suitcase." Shannon put his hand up under the sling. There was a little blood, no pain. He could almost feel the slug, it was so close to the skin. The impact had even shocked all the ache out of his broken arm. It was numb.

Gus Vogel came in with Fran McGowan. She looked at Shannon's face, went to her knees beside his chair. "Oh, Shan, Shan, are you hurt?"

He nodded dully. I've been hurt for a long time, kitten. Ever since they found my skipper dead in an alley. I guess maybe he'll feel better now. I don't know."

"Of course he will, Shan," she said, humoring him. "Of course he will." She looked sort of helplessly at Vogel.

Gus came over, put his derby on the desk, looked at a pudgy hand. He slapped Shannon with the hand. Hard. Then he said, "Excuse me, John J."

The dullness went out of Shannon's eyes. "Why, you pot-bellied Dutch bastard! I'll—" Then he grinned, crookedly, but as though he was in his right mind again. "Remind me to kick you in the pants some time, will you, Gus?"

Vogel nodded happily. O'Meara went to the door, let in a couple of dicks, jerked his head at the still unconscious Regan. "Take him away some place."

Argyle, who had opened the suitcase, was clucking his tongue over a small memo book bound in limp morocco. There were some pass books, too. He tossed the memo book to O'Meara. "That ought to help you sort out the sheep from the goats. He had quite a tight little organization." His lips moved soundlessly, totalling some of the entries in the pass books. "Hmm-m-m. Imagine this. Well for Christ's sake!"

O'Meara looked at Shannon. "How did you know?"

"I didn't. I just knew my skipper, is all. I knew him inside and out. I finally got around to thinking about how far he would go for a friend, and Regan leaving town on the eve of election—well, it gave me an idea. Say it was Regan, not you, who was crooked. Say the skipper found it out. Maybe he even had those little books to prove it. But Regan was his friend, get it? He wouldn't let Regan go on, but he would give him a chance to get away.

"Regan pretended to go away. He flew to San Francisco. Then he came back, secretly. He wanted what the skipper had. While he was looking for it the skipper caught him and was killed. Regan couldn't find the stuff.

"Rattled, he went to his pal, Big Nick Lombardi. Lombardi already had Duquesne's five-grand check, for another purpose—to run Duquesne out of town on a frame that hadn't been plotted yet. This was the golden opportunity, now. Instead of just running Duquesne out of town he could be railroaded to the lethal chamber.

"I think that Regan at some time must have visited Duquesne and lifted the gun, not for any special purpose, perhaps, but just in case. That was the gun Regan used on the skipper. Duquesne probably remembered Regan's visit, suspected who had taken the gun. That's why he tried to get Regan tonight at the airport. He was a funny guy, Floyd Duquesne. He never said much, but I guess he could hate like the rest of us.

"Anyway, Lombardi and Regan went back and jobbed the skipper and Duquesne both at the same time by planting Duquesne's check on the skipper's corpse. Regan flew north again to the convention, even made his scheduled speech this morning. After he made it he sneaked back to search some more. Lombardi was searching too, with no success. Between them they figured that I might have it, or know about it, because I was close to the skipper.

"That's why I was bombed last night in the police garage. Regan could have had that done through some of his clique on the inside. It would be simple enough. When that didn't work, Lombardi tried to get at me in another way. Maybe he even figured on crossing Regan, afraid that Regan would squeal if caught. I don't know. Nobody will even know now, I guess. It's even possible that Lombardi figured Duquesne would go after Regan at the airport tonight when he made his official return to town, and sent Sticky out to do something about it."

"What the hell?" O'Meara grinned. "They're all dead, aren't they?"

"That's one way of looking at it," Shannon said. "I still feel lousy about Duquesne, though. He was a square guy and deserved a hell of a lot better deal than this town even gave him."

Paul Shacklewood Argyle closed his lips firmly. "He was a gambler. Good or bad, it's better that he's gone." He took off his glasses, pointed them at Shannon. "You still haven't shown us proof that Regan kept moving back and forth between here and San Francisco."

"I can," Shannon assured him. "I've got a hacker named Osterwicz who saw him in Captain Grady's house this afternoon. I have airplane pilots, despatchers, field crews, stewardesses and even a key-pounder who will plot out the courses he took, both on the regular airlines and the independent non-scheduled flights. This afternoon, when he finally located what he wanted in the skipper's house, he sneaked up to Santa Barbara and from there he wired you that he was coming in at ten. All along, he pretended he wanted me on his side to help him clean things up. Actually he was keeping an eye on me in case I knew anything or discovered anything. When he had the stuff himself, he knew it was time to blot me out for good. He tried, and failed. With all these things, and the books you're holding in your hands, if District Attorney Jorgensen can't get a conviction against Regan I'll finish beating him to death and enjoy it."

O'Meara coughed gently. "I guess we had our wires crossed, Shannon. I knew there was something wrong and Regan going out of town gave me my chance. From where I sat you looked like you were in it up to your neck. I had to play rough."

"Okay," Shannon grunted. "I thought the same about you so that makes us even."

Mayor Argyle cleared his throat. "And you'll come back to the force now, Shannon? There's a promotion waiting for you."

"Hell!" Shannon grinned. "I was never off it!"

"And you damned well better behave," O'Meara said. "No more of this wild man stuff. What the hell did you have to shoot Lombardi for anyway?"

"Because he would have shot me."

"No," OMeara said. "Don't kid me. You went there intending to kill him."

"All right, maybe I did." Shannon shrugged, moved over to Fran McGowan and put his good arm around her. "Christ, we've just proved there aren't any wings on a cop. The son of a bitch picked on my girl."

THE END

TO THE READER

If you enjoyed this book, you will be glad to know that there are many others just as well written, just as interesting, to be had in the Fiction House Press Library.

You will find the Fiction House Press Library online at

www.FictionHousePress.com

www.ingramcontent.com/pod-product-compliance
Lightning Source LLC
LaVergne TN
LVHW091007080826
845145LV00003B/1159

* 9 7 8 1 6 4 7 2 0 6 2 1 5 *